None of the Above

The Dial Press · New York

None of the Above

Rosemary Wells

F
WEL

Library of Congress Cataloging in Publication Data
Wells, Rosemary. None of the above.
I. Title.
PZ7.W46843NO [Fic] 74-2879
ISBN 0-8037-6148-1

For my Editor, P. J. F.

Contents

Thirteen *3*

Fourteen *25*

Fifteen *59*

Sixteen *89*

Seventeen *154*

Eighteen *175*

None of the Above

Thirteen

"Marcia Mill is a big fat pill," said Christina Van Dam in not a particularly low voice.

Mother was washing a head of lettuce. She gave her a warning look.

"But it isn't fair. Johnny, tell her it isn't fair!" Christina turned to her older brother. "It's been three weeks now and all she does is eat candy and watch television and chew chewing gum."

"Is that what you want to do?" Mother asked. "Watch 'The Dating Game' in the middle of the afternoon?"

"No, but . . . "

"No buts. I'm doing the best I can with Marcia. You can't make a silk purse out of a sow's ear. Not overnight anyway."

Marcia heard all this through the floor of her bedroom. She had no certain reaction to what they said. At least, if she had, it was safely hidden in a deep, calm pool inside her. Marcia liked picturing this pool. It was reassuring.

She could remember three, maybe four stultifying Sunday afternoons in this house when her mother and Mr. Van Dam were both still alive. Her father had been acquainted with Mr. Van Dam in the navy, or perhaps they had grown up in the same town—she couldn't recall. The memory of the Sunday visits was cloudy and mixed up with other Sundays at other people's houses. It was always either too hot or too cold for her to go outdoors, and so she stayed in and allowed the adult chatter to lull her like the motion of a train. Chrissy and John Van Dam, with whom she had been encouraged to go and play, were animated people. Chrissy was her own age, but she seemed alternately much older or younger, depending on what she was doing. Chrissy was not a bit like Marcia's friends in New Bedford. Marcia was neither curious, nor bothered by her. She simply ignored her the way she did difficult math problems at school. "I'd father stay here, thanks," was all it took to make Chrissy go flying out the door, quite relieved. There was generally no more discussion, unless Mrs. Van Dam put in a word about swimming or playing in the snow being healthy, to which Marcia and her family never replied.

Marcia got up from her bed and went downstairs silently. She sat next to the fireplace, where it was warm.

"The woodman cometh!" John shouted in her direction. Marcia looked up. John was smiling at her. "Penny for your thoughts," he said, allowing an armful of soaking wet pine logs to crash on the hearth.

"What? I'm sorry," Marcia answered automatically. John was almost always saying things she couldn't understand, probably because he was in college.

"Got to put you to work, that's the Puritan way!" he said,

and laughed. "Hey, how would you like to be firewarden for the week?"

"Sure."

John kicked the snow off his boots as he tramped upstairs. His parka dripped a muddy river all the way from the kitchen.

"What do you want me to do?" Marcia called up after him.

"Oh, just throw a log on now and then. Don't let the fire get too low!" he yelled back.

For a minute Marcia stared at the fire. They had had no fireplace in their old house. The Van Dam's house was much bigger. That was why they had to move in when her father married Mrs. Van Dam. The house was filled with other things they had not had at home: the polished maple colonial furniture, the bookcases, the books. . . . She placed a short pudgy index finger on one of the logs. Her finger was not at all in the same order of things as a rough piece of pine. John's hands were big and brown and almost looked as if they were made of wood themselves. She didn't want to touch the dirty log. She was afraid the fire might spatter out onto the rug if she meddled with it. It would throw sparks. The whole house could go up in flames.

Marcia was unsure of so many things in the house—fire, for instance. Of course she had seen fireplaces before, but weren't they afraid the roof might catch? Her mother would never have taken that chance. Something in the pattern of the wallpaper reminded her of her mother's face. She jumped a little because she had been unable to visualize it for six months or so and felt guilty. The image was as clear as a photograph, but when she looked closer it vanished and became a cluster of leaves and acorns again. It shouldn't be in the wallpaper of this house, Marcia told herself. Mr. Van Dam's face yes; it had been his house. She looked back for a minute to see if he too was peering out at her, but she couldn't remember at all what Mr. Van Dam had looked like.

The firelight danced teasingly over every bright surface in the room. "World's Greatest Literature," Marcia read to herself. She imagined the flames consuming the enormous set of leatherbound volumes from Aristotle through Zola. Every thing burned very quickly in her thoughts, even the tarragon— whatever that was—which was being argued about in the kitchen. When the fire was over, she and her father and her sister would wrap themselves in blankets and go to the police station, trampling through the snow saying it was too bad everything had to burn down. The police would be nice, maybe they would even give her candy. Then, perhaps, she could go down to Florida and live with Aunt Jane for a while.

"Too much tarragon—you're putting too much tarragon in!" objected Mother.

"Mother, it's a cheese dressing," Chrissy answered. "You can't taste anything else in a cheese dressing anyway. I don't know why you want me to put it in at all."

"It's what the recipe calls for," Mother said in a final sort of voice.

So they were putting the cheese with the mold into the salad again. The thought made Marcia's stomach turn. She wouldn't eat it. That was that. Mold could kill you. Her father wouldn't speak up about it. He paid no attention whatever to the preparation of meals but simply ate what was put before him. Marcia had gotten used to the TV dinners her sister made for them every night since her mother had died. She liked them. They reminded her of lunches on airplanes when she'd gone down to visit Aunt Jane. Marcia had been on a plane six times in her life. She wondered if Chrissy had ever flown. If not, that was one area where she had Chrissy clearly beaten, but she didn't dare ask for fear of finding yet another thing that Chrissy had done a hundred times or else didn't care about at all.

Bang! Stamp! Somebody new was in the kitchen. It was Jennifer, a friend of Chrissy's.

Mother said, "Take those things off. No, throw them in the laundry room. It's hot in there and they'll dry. You'll catch your death!"

"Cold! Wow! El Frigettorio out there!" Jenny's quick voice shouted. "Sometimes I hate Massachusetts. I wish we'd move to Hawaii or something."

"Nonsense, Jenny," Mother said. "Hawaii's awful. All that hot, sticky weather and the most terrible people retire there. You couldn't ski in Hawaii anyway. Aren't you girls going to Sunapee tomorrow?"

Sunapee was another word like Zola, or tarragon. Marcia had seen skiing, all right. People swooping down a mountain like maniacs, even adults, in the freezing cold and wet . . . broken bones, not for her, thank you. There were better things to fill a Saturday afternoon—movies, for one.

"God bless New Eng-e-land / Land that I love / Stand beside her / And guide her / Through the night / With a light / From a bulb." Jennifer and Chrissy burst into peals of laughter at their private joke song.

"You girls!" said Mother, also laughing. "Come on now, Chrissy, finish up with the salad. Jenny, go stand by the fire for a few minutes and warm up and then you can help mash the potatoes."

"Marcia, hi!" Jenny was suddenly standing next to her, red faced and out of breath from her walk. Quick long fingers drew a chapstick out of a woolly pocket.

"Hi," Marcia said. Now she remembered Jenny's face better. Front row, third seat—next to Chrissy in the advanced eighth grade. Marcia was in the B section.

"How do you like school?" Jenny asked after an uncomfortable moment of silence.

"Fine, I guess."

"Joined any clubs yet?"

"Nope."

More silence.

"Gee," Jenny observed. Marcia picked some lint off the front of her sweater.

"Warming up, Jenny?" Mother asked from the kitchen.

"Yes, Mrs. Van Dam. Are the potatoes ready for me yet?"

"It's Mill now," said Mother. "Mrs. Mill."

"Oops, sorry."

"Two more minutes and the potatoes will be ready."

"Okay." Jenny did not say Mrs. Mill. She asked Marcia, "Um, shouldn't there be another log on this fire? It's going out."

"Marcia's supposed to put it on," shouted Chrissy.

Jenny looked for an explanation. Marcia shrugged. "It's very heavy," she said.

"Heavy!" Jenny dropped two logs neatly on the fire.

"I was afraid. I mean I didn't want to start a fire on the rug and if—"

"Jenny, Marcia's supposed to do that," Chrissy interrupted. "I heard John tell her she was firewarden this week." Chrissy was suddenly in the room.

"What does it matter?" Jenny asked.

"It matters because everybody has their jobs," said Chrissy primly. "Hey, Marcia, you want to trade with me? I'll do the fire if you set the table."

"Okay," said Marcia slowly, knowing she'd been trapped but not knowing exactly how.

"Well, you better go set it then. Dinner's in five minutes," said Chrissy when Marcia didn't get up.

Marcia wandered into the kitchen. She took seven knives and seven forks out of the drawer. Seven silver napkin rings. She wondered if other utensils were needed. She decided to take out the spoons just in case.

"Two forks, no spoons," said Mother from the other side of the kitchen. That meant there was to be no dessert again. Mother was on a diet, although she wasn't fat at all. Marcia supposed she was overweight, but she had always been told she was pretty. People admired her sky blue eyes and her natural blond hair, and although she wouldn't be fourteen until May, she was already developing a nicely rounded figure, she thought, especially compared to Chrissy, who was as wiry and flat-chested as Marcia was plump. Mother, however, thought Marcia was fat and had said so almost the first day, not in so many words, of course, just something about "all of us losing weight together!" Marcia sighed. She and Mother had a dreadful time talking together, but Mother had the advantage of being a grown-up and therefore could say whatever she pleased. Being one of "them" was also an advantage.

"Them," to Marcia, was something you were or were not; there was no changing it. It involved skiing and horseback riding and books, and little things like tarragon. It meant you were thin and smart, and sometimes rich, but money wasn't all of it by a long shot. Money didn't make them unglassy-eyed, unpudgy, didn't give them long talented fingers and straight white teeth. Marcia's allowance was three times what Chrissy got, but she and her sister would never be like any of the Van Dams. Her sister, Sharon, was upstairs at this very moment, taking her rollers out, but her hair would always be oily, no matter what creme rinses and shampoos she used, and despite the medications she bought for her face, it was always swarming with carefully hidden blemishes. "Here comes the Clearasil personality of the month," Chrissy had whispered to Mother one night last week when Sharon appeared wearing an unusually thick coat of makeup. Marcia had burned at this, but Sharon didn't care. Sharon was eighteen and getting married in June. She was safe.

For the three weeks they had all lived together, dinner had been a silent affair. Marcia and Sharon never said much, and their father just concentrated on eating. But now that John was home for his midwinter break, and Jenny was there too, dinner was very lively. John didn't make Marcia feel uncomfortable, however. He never tried to draw her into conversation by introducing formal topics. Marcia liked him.

He even twitted his thin, piano playing, athletic sister about her English teacher. "How's Mary Queen of Scots doing?" he asked.

"Don't call her that, Johnny. She's nice," said Chrissy.

"She gave me B's. The only B's I ever got in grammar school."

"Well, you probably didn't work."

"What are you reading in English now?" Mother broke in.

"*A Tale of Two Cities,*" Chrissy said, "and tonight I have to write a short story."

"What are you reading in English, Marcia?" Mother turned her head to face the other side of the table.

"I don't know. I forget." Marcia answered.

"*Ivanhoe.* Their class has *Ivanhoe,* condensed version of course," said Chrissy.

"Oh, yeah. I forgot. She just gave it to us Friday."

"*Ivanhoe!* How nice!" said Mother, and turning back to Chrissy once again, she said, "A short story you're to make up yourself?" Mother looked pleased. Miss Kosky, Chrissy's teacher, was Scottish, although heaven knows how she came to have the name Kosky. She was a subject of great interest to Mother because of her accent, which was marvelous, and because she encouraged "creativity" in her students.

"What's your short story about?" John asked.

"Harlem," said Chrissy, taking a gulp of milk.

Marcia's father raised his head quizzically.

"Harlem!" John almost shouted. "What do you know about Harlem?"

"I know a lot more than you think, Mr. Smarty."

"Have you ever been to Harlem?"

"No, but that doesn't mean I can't write about what I feel. Miss Kosky says we're supposed to write about what we feel and I feel strongly about Harlem. I even have my opening sentence."

"Your opening sentence?"

"Yup. That's the most important part of a short story," Chrissy explained. "You give the key to the story in the opening sentence. Otherwise, people will stop reading."

"So what's your opening sentence?"

"If you think . . . If you think it's easy being a Negro, you're wrong," she recited.

John covered his face with his napkin.

"Black," said Mother, "you should say black, not Negro."

"Okay . . . black, then. But I don't see what's so terrible," said Chrissy. There were tears in her voice. Marcia felt impatient at Chrissy's explosive crying. It was always somewhere, just under the surface. Marcia herself could not remember the last time she had cried. A hearse, swollen and gleaming, as if it were itself diseased, pierced her memory until she blotted it out.

Sharon ate slowly, her eyes stationed on Chrissy. The subject of black people had arisen once before at dinner. Marcia's father had said that there had been many more "coloreds" in the New Bedford school than there were here in Gloucester— the school had been half full of them. Somewhere, Marcia knew, there was a rule that said there was to be no arguing at dinner. Her father's statement had been greeted by a precise silence. Marcia hoped Sharon would not say anything now. She also hoped John would not ask her about opening sentences or short stories. She was happy her class was writing business and friendly letters instead, but she didn't want John to know.

Marcia and Sharon shared the largest bedroom in the house. Some signal must have been given out by Sharon because Mother and Chrissy seldom came in. Marcia was careful to keep it neat. She even cleaned up after her sister so there would be no criticism.

Sharon called Mother "Sparky" behind her back. It was her real nickname, but she insisted the two girls call her "Mother." Sharon had settled on "you." Marcia had a bit more trouble. She had tried to explain that her real mother was dead and that she didn't think she could. It didn't sound right.

"But what else are you going to call me, dear?" Mother had asked. Marcia had not thought about this.

"I don't know," she mumbled.

"I think you could give it a try. I don't think your mother would have minded too much. As a matter of fact, I'm positive she'd want you to."

"I'd rather call you Sparky, or Alberta, even."

"You can't do that, Marcia. You're not old enough. Only grown-ups call other grown-ups by their first names. Now don't you worry. You'll get used to it after a while."

Sharon had also told Marcia not to worry, that once she and Buddy were married, Marcia could come and live with them. Sharon was sure their father would not last six months in his new marriage.

"Dad'd never get a divorce," Marcia said. "He doesn't believe in divorce. Besides, you can see how he's changed since
. . . that whole time after Mamma died, and when she was sick.
I almost thought he was going to die too. I really think
he's . . . well, happy again. You have to admit that, Shar.
Even with the arguments. They never argue about anything
except you and me, anyway."

"Umph," Sharon answered, her mouth full of hair clips,
"if that b-i-t-c-h didn't make me take all my rollers out for
dinner, I wouldn't have to go to the trouble of putting up my
hair all over again."

Marcia settled herself on the bed with a pile of movie magazines. "I could never come and live with you and Buddy,"
she said, leafing through the top one.

"You could if I said so," said Sharon fiercely. "Besides, old
Sparks would probably love to have you off her back."

"But what about Daddy? I couldn't leave Daddy."

"Like I said, honey. It ain't gonna last."

Marcia had her doubts, however. She generally kept her
opinions of people to a minimum, but she didn't like Buddy
very much. He was always coming up and touching her sister,
on the arm, on the cheek, and when Sharon wasn't there, he did
it to any female who happened to be in the room. He came
so close to her, Marcia could smell his aftershave. Buddy never
went without a tie, and his shirts had funny, woven designs
in the material. Marcia had once seen the contents of his
wallet. What appeared to be hundreds of bills were folded in
a gold money clip. His skin was olive colored, and he drove a
big red Camaro and was "real Italian looking," as Sharon
put it. Chrissy had observed, more than once, that he looked
like a member of the mob, but Sharon told her not to listen
to Chrissy, who was just jealous anyhow because Buddy looked

exactly like Perry Como. Her father . . . but then her father
was so tolerant. "It takes all kinds," he was fond of saying.
Still, Marcia worried about her sister marrying into the mob.

Sunapee was two hours away. Chrissy and Jennifer left at
seven in the morning. While Marcia was still half asleep, she
listened to the clatter of boots, skis, and breakfast dishes. She
allowed herself to wake very slowly, careful not to move a
muscle, ignoring an itchy wisp of hair on her face. Some morn-
ings she could separate her mind from the rest of her body
and allow it to float over the sounds that came through the
floor. Her flights seldom took her to fanciful places. It was
enough if she could make her fat, constant form evaporate for
a while. This time she wished herself back to the attic of their
old house, where she could sit, unprodded, for hours and watch
the street through the cobwebs on the window. She managed
to do this for about twenty minutes until Chrissy rapped
loudly on the door and said, "Mom says to get up!"

Sharon lay in bed like a lump of clay. She wouldn't get
up until it suited her. Marcia knew she had about ten minutes
before Mother herself came in after her, and that, of course,
would start the day off very badly. Mother believed in early
rising, big breakfasts, and open windows. Marcia decided
to give in as much as possible this morning because she wanted
to go to White's with her new friend Lynn this afternoon, and
there might be a battle involved.

She dressed carefully and appeared downstairs just as Chrissy
and Jennifer were piling into the station wagon parked in the
driveway. Jennifer's whole family went skiing almost every
weekend, it seemed. They all tramped out in the freezing cold,
carrying tons of lumpy equipment, and risked their very lives
on some remote mountain that might as well have been the
North Pole. To Marcia it was as bad as camping, if not worse.

She knew people did these things and lived to tell about them but she couldn't believe they did them on purpose. Things were not as bad as they could have been, however. Mother didn't ski and didn't insist that Marcia go with Chrissy.

"A little coffee in your milk?"

Marcia was startled. Coffee was forbidden, not as much as eye makeup or rollers at the dinner table, because Mother herself drank a great deal of coffee. For children it was out because it was simply bad for you.

"Yes, please."

Mother smiled efficiently. A plate of eggs appeared before Marcia. Mother sat down and crossed her legs under the kitchen counter. Marcia began to eat without looking at her plate.

"Well, seeing you're not doing anything today, would you like to come shopping with me?" Mother asked briskly.

"Uh . . . okay."

"That didn't sound too enthusiastic."

"Huh?"

"Enthusiastic. You don't have to if you don't want to, Marcia."

"Well, it's just that Lynn's coming over and we were going to go over to White's."

"White's! You went there last Saturday and the Saturday before!"

Marcia had got through her whole fried egg without gagging. She started wordlessly on the white of the second one.

"Marcia?"

"Yeah?"

"Please don't say 'huh' or 'yeah.' "

"Yes."

"I thought maybe as a surprise we could go to Jordan's and buy you a ski outfit."

"Okay, I guess."

"Marcia, if you don't want a ski outfit, just say so. I asked your father and he said, 'Fine, buy whatever you like.' We have a charge at Jordan's now and I thought it might be fun if you tried some on. The parkas and pants are lovely colors this year."

"I don't want one, thank you," Marcia mumbled.

"Don't you think it would be nice to try some sport?"

The second yolk stared up at Marcia like an awful eye. "I go bowling," she said.

"Bowling isn't a sport, it's just— First of all I meant something outdoors."

"Daddy goes bowling."

"I wasn't talking about your father. I was talking about you."

"I guess I'm just not the type," said Marcia after a pause.

Mother almost tossed the breakfast dishes into the sink. "I guess you're not," she said.

Marcia broke the yolk of her second egg and smeared it around the rim of her plate, trying to make it look as if it had been eaten. "Where's Daddy?" she asked.

"Having the car fixed."

"Do you want me to do any chores?"

"Look at your list."

Marcia groped in a drawer. Half of Chrissy's chores were checked. She would probably do the rest Sunday. John was back in college, but he didn't have to do chores anyway. Sharon seldom did hers, but Mother never argued with Sharon, just with their father about Sharon. Marcia was supposed to clean the downstairs bathroom. She put her plate very quickly into the dishwasher so as to avoid another egg argument.

"Should I do a couple of Chrissy's chores this morning?"

"Chrissy can take care of her own chores. Just take care of yours."

"I was going to."

Marcia took a sponge and cleaner out from under the sink.

"Can I still go to White's?"

"Ask your father."

"I don't have to ask Daddy. He already gave me some money and he doesn't mind if I go."

"Then I guess you can go."

Mother stood polishing the never-used Van Dam family silver. Her face was tight and angry around her mouth. A lock of gray hair kept falling over her eye, and she pushed it back severely, as if it were responsible for her mood. Chrissy had said that Mother turned completely gray the week after Mr. Van Dam had died. The first evening Marcia had spent in the house Chrissy had confided to her that the morning after the funeral Mother had come downstairs, her face and hair completely gray and ever after her hair had remained so. Sharon didn't believe this story when Marcia had repeated it to her. "She just forget to dye it, I bet," was Sharon's explanation.

Marcia and Lynn bought sno-cones at the entrance to White's. The entire department store spread out before them on one floor. It appeared to vibrate slightly in the blue-white light that came from no definable source. Marcia squinted at the ceiling for a moment, but the upper air was so filled with cigarette smoke and blinding fluorescence that she had to look down, and the lower air was so choked with the smell of hot dogs and ever-bubbling orange-drink machines that she could hardly breathe. Still, it was warm, and there were thousands of items to be bought dirt cheap and thousands of people to watch.

Marcia and Lynn tried on sweaters for a while. When they came out of the dressing room, Lynn whispered, "Will you look at that one!"

A gangly, clubfooted boy, who could have been twelve or thirty-five, stared dociley at his mother's back as she rummaged through the apron counter. His hair was crewcut and grew in little whorls and his mouth hung open loosely. Marcia gave Lynn a punch in the arm, and they both dashed out of earshot into the sportswear department to laugh. They followed the mother and the boy from aprons to shoes to portable heaters, bursting into peals of silent laughter every time the mother said, "Come along, Robert!" Once she turned to glare at them, but there was too much noise and too many people for her to say anything.

Lynn bought a bracelet with six turtle charms. Marcia spent most of her money on a day-glo pink angora sweater and a Bambi pin. Lynn approved these purchases heartily and said she wished she had as good an allowance as Marcia.

"It's because Mamma died. Daddy thinks he should make it up to me because of Mamma," Marcia explained.

The possibility of her own mother's death resulting in such consequences flickered briefly over Lynn's face. "I'm hungry," she said.

"I hardly have any more money. I have only a dollar and thirty cents," said Marcia.

"That's plenty. You can get a hot dog and french fries."

Marcia knew that. She was thinking of Mother and dinner and Mother's probable reaction to day-glo pink.

"Come on, I want something anyway," said Lynn.

Marcia sighed and eased herself into a seat across from Lynn.

"Canucks!" whispered Lynn.

"What?"

"Listen."

Marcia could make out that there was a conversation in French going on in the booth behind them. Workers from Canada, probably, she thought.

"Abba dabba dabba," said Lynn, giggling.

"*Tant pis,*" said the man to his wife.

"Tompee," said Lynn.

"Tompee Tompee, Madame de Paris!" said Marcia loudly. The man turned around. He was unshaven and had a scar on his lip. Marcia almost spilled the ice-cream sundae she had ordered. When he turned back to his family, they both had to hold their noses to keep their laughing down.

Marcia didn't know whether Mother and Chrissy disapproved of her new sweater and pin or if they had simply not noticed. After all, she did have another day-glo pink angora sweater, but it was a cardigan. Chrissy was angry because she wanted to be allowed to go to Jenny's house for dinner and then to the movies. "Saturday night you do your homework if you haven't done it Friday," Mother told her sharply.

Chrissy groaned. "Yeah. Me and who else?"

"Never mind about that and don't start picking up that 'yeah' business. Before you know it you'll start speaking as if you came from a slum."

Marcia waited until this exchange was over. Then she went in to set the table. In the middle of dinner Mother asked her suddenly, "Marcia, do you have any homework?"

"Some. I'll do it."

"Tonight, please."

"But there's a quiz show on."

"You may watch television after you do your homework."

"But it'll be over by then. It's at eight."

"If Chrissy can't watch television neither can you. We cannot have unfair situations."

"Daddy, do I have to?" Marcia asked.

"Marcia," Mother continued, "your father wants you to be just as much my daughter as Chrissy is. Please try to cooperate."

Marcia's father cleared his throat. "Look, Sparky," he said, "why don't you let both girls watch TV. We don't have to have all these hard-and-fast rules."

"I don't want to watch stupid old TV," said Chrissy.

"Don't tell me you want to do your homework," he said in innocent surprise. "I heard you say before you wanted to go to the movies with Jenny."

"Well, Mom says no, and if I get my homework done I can go to see *The Lion in Winter* tomorrow night. Who wants to watch stupid dumb old TV programs anyway?"

"Well, that should settle it," said Mother with an expression of relief. "Marcia, if you finish your homework you can go with Chrissy tomorrow night. We'll all go. I'd love to see *The Lion in Winter*."

"*Hello Dolly!* is playing at Cinema Two," said Marcia.

"Majority rules," said Chrissy.

"Why can't you all go to see that animal movie and I'll just go to the other theater," said Marcia. "They're right together and the shows start about the same time."

"Marcia," said Mother tightly, "You can't go into the movies alone. You don't want to be bothered by some horrible man, do you? Besides, it's not an animal movie at all, if that's what's worrying you. It's all about a king and queen of England, way back hundreds of years ago. They say it's a marvelous movie."

"History!" Marcia said hopelessly.

"It might be good for you to learn some history," said Chrissy. "Even though the General Course probably doesn't even touch on English history because its too hard."

Sharon stopped eating and raised her head for the first time. "You lay off her," she said barely audibly.

"Hey! She can talk!" Chrissy piped back. "I didn't know she'd learned."

"Both of you, leave the table!" said Mother.

Marcia, Mother, and her father all finished dinner in silence. When her father placed his fork and knife neatly beside his plate and stared over Mother's head into the kitchen, Marcia felt something in her stomach hurt. She couldn't remember the last time he had been angry. "All that was unnecessary," he said. "We don't have to have fights. . . . "

"We should straighten things out," said Mother. "We wouldn't have disagreements if everybody agreed on the same things."

Marcia leaned closer to her father. She couldn't leave her body, as she had done that morning, and float over this conversation. She was afraid she would be sick in another moment.

"Nobody ever agrees all the time on the same things," her father went on. "It's humanly impossible to—"

"I didn't *say* everyone should agree all the time. Of *course* that's impossible," Mother interrupted. "All I'm saying is that everybody should cooperate."

Marcia's father said nothing to that. He realigned his knife and fork. Was he listening now? Marcia didn't know. She excused herself from the table and cleared the plates away, carefully.

"Thank you, Marcia," said Mother suddenly.

"What?"

"For excusing yourself. You remembered." Then she turned back to Marcia's father and said, "Charles, please. How do you expect me to raise the girls as my own if you constantly fight me on it? You wanted me to do it. Now I'm trying and I'm getting no help at all."

Marcia closed the heavy swinging door, but she could still hear bits of the conversation. Mother's words broke off and turned to sobs. She, Marcia, had been the cause of all this.

Maybe she should think about moving in with Sharon and Buddy. Her father's voice was low now, and she could make out only a few words like "difficult" and "takes time."

She cleaned up the sink. Better than Chrissy ever does it, she told herself as she polished the chrome so that it gleamed. She recalled her own mother's instructions on this matter. She had made some reference to the "kitchen of the future," which she had seen once at the 1939 World's Fair. Marcia had been encouraged to clean the kitchen as if it were to be on display in a world's fair. Mother walked into the kitchen suddenly. Her eyes were dry and her voice was firm and cheerful.

"Your father and I have worked this out a little better now, Marcia. I'm sorry there was such a fuss."

Marcia didn't dare ask if she might watch television. She couldn't think of anything appropriate to say. Mother snapped up a dish towel and began vigorously to dry the already dry dishes. "It's been hard on all of us," said Mother.

Marcia still didn't reply.

"But I'm sure it will all work out, given a little time. These things take time."

She was quoting Marcia's father, Marcia knew that, somehow, and was pleased. "Can I ask a question?" she said, surprising herself.

"Of course."

"Do you love my father as much as Mr. Van Dam?"

"As much, Marcia, but in a different way."

Marcia had heard this somewhere before. She wished she had not blurted out that question.

"Mr. Van Dam was very dear to me," Mother went on. "He was a different sort of person from your father. I think you love everybody in a different way, don't you?"

"I guess so." Marcia started to leave the kitchen.

"Marcia, please come back."

Marcia stopped in the doorway and looked at Mother with as neutral an expression as she could manage.

"I hope . . . I hope you know I would like to feel about you just the way I do about Chrissy, and this may be very hard to understand, but I want . . . I want it to be the same between your father and me as it was with . . . with Mr. Van Dam. Chrissy and you are very different from each other and it's hard . . . it's difficult with two families. Your father and I knew there'd be problems, and well, you've just been here a few weeks now and I'm sure things will be fine if . . . "

"Sure," said Marcia.

"Do you . . . do you still miss your own mother very much?"

"I guess I do."

"Well," said Mother, looking away suddenly, "I'd like to think you'll . . . well, you'll talk to me if anything bothers you. And I think . . . I think you'll probably miss her less as times goes by. We . . . your father's setting up the slide projector. Our honeymoon slides from Europe came back. If you'd like to see them, maybe you can do your homework later or tomorrow."

"Okay."

"Why don't you call Chrissy and Sharon down?" Mother said brightly.

"Okay."

The Bridge of Sighs, Mother explained, was named in such a way because prisoners in seventeenth-century Venice had had their last look at the world from that very bridge before they were executed, and they had apparently sighed a great deal in the process. On the screen in the darkened living room Mother beamed from the Bridge of Sighs.

She beamed from the steps of Saint Peter's and from the Ghiberti doors in Florence. She and Marcia's father held hands and clasped flowers on a quai next to the Seine. An obliging fellow from Minneapolis had taken that picture, her father explained. In a café with a pristine white tablecloth before them and a pastry table to the side, they clinked wine glasses and smiled, Marcia noticed, so terribly lovingly at each other. Marcia wished Sharon had come down for the show. It proved that she, Marcia, had been right about their father. He looked like a schoolboy on holiday in all the pictures. The two of them, in their private adult way, had enjoyed themselves, she could see that. She looked at the faces, both of them grinning broadly on either side of a Beefeater, and although she didn't know the words for exactly what she meant, she sensed the desperate joy in their expressions, and she guessed that Mother had probably gone through an ordeal not unlike her father's— terror and loneliness and tears kept from the children so as not to distress them further.

Fourteen

"I wish Mamma could have lived to see my wedding day,"
said Sharon, sighing dramatically as she wound her wet blond
hair in even coils and clipped it to her rollers.

Marcia sat down heavily on her sister's unmade bed. She
nodded in agreement but at the same time remembered that
Sharon had fought incessantly with their mother before her
death, and most of the fighting had to do with Buddy. He
drove too fast and his friends looked "suspicious." He was not
dependable and Sharon should be on the lookout for a solid
husband, not a practical joker with a reputation for being fast
with girls. Their real mother had been more vociferous on the
point than Chrissy or Mother, who would have agreed whole-
heartedly, but who tried to keep their opinions to themselves
out of politeness.

"I said if only Mamma could have been alive for my wedding day," Sharon repeated, looking at Marcia this time.

"I know," Marcia managed to answer without choking on her words. She had fears for her sister but more for herself, not the least of them being that she was about to cry, and she couldn't remember the last time she had lost control. That very day Sharon would desert her. She, Marcia, was maid of honor, which was a gratifying thing to be, but later that afternoon Sharon would drive away in Buddy's big red Camaro and the day would all be over. The pink organza dress would have to be rehung in the closet where it was now waiting in a plastic bag for the short ceremony. It seemed unfair to Marcia that Sharon had chosen to go off with a man and leave her alone to live in this room that did not yet feel like her own. Marcia did not question the fact that boyfriends and engagements were exciting. Weddings and showers and honeymoons were what every girl wanted—more than anything, she sensed—to show off to other girl friends and feel important and secret over. But the day-to-day meanness of living with a man, cleaning up after his breakfast, and hoping he would not come home exhausted at night—all these things Marcia had seen her mother live, and the thought of Sharon wanting to live them puzzled her. Besides, she wanted to tell Sharon that she, Marcia, was worth more loyalty than that. The two of them were all that was left after their mother's death (somehow their father didn't count because of his remarriage). For that reason alone it was right that they stay together. But there were no arguments to be marshaled against a diamond ring and those hushed, giggling conversations her sister had on the telephone with her friends. Marcia assumed that one day, if she were to be stumbled upon by some man wanting a wife, she too would marry, but the yawning future between now and that far-off state threatened her, and some dull, soft thought in the back of her mind prevented her sister's wedding-day headiness from ringing quite true.

Suddenly she wept silently and hopelessly on the bed, not reaching out for Sharon until her sister turned and saw tears splattering down on the maid of honor bouquet and came over with a wad of Kleenex. Crying made Marcia feel fat. "I'm so ugly!" she said inexplicably to her sister.

"You're not!" snapped Sharon. "You'll get married too someday. Now don't mess up those flowers. Honestly!" She thrust the Kleenex at Marcia, who blew her nose stuffily. "Why do you think you're ugly? Has Sparky been after you with her diets again?"

"Yes," said Marcia, breaking into more tears because this was not exactly true.

"Well, just don't *listen* to that crap, honey! I told you she's just jealous because Chrissy is so flat-chested. You'll marry somebody just as cute as Buddy. Buddy thinks you're real pretty. He told me so."

"That's nice," said Marcia shakily, regaining a little control and swiping at her eyes and nose. She was not sure if she was pleased about Buddy's compliment. She had grown to like him less and less over the past seven months. Seven months, to be sure, spent listening to Mother and Chrissy drop little hints of what they thought about Buddy. But her own observation warned her as well about things she did not like to admit. One day she had been crossing a street when a car roared out of a gas station. A wife, pale and frightened, sat in the front seat next to her husband, and three children bounced around in back. The car was battered and spewed blue exhaust. It was old enough to have cloth instead of vinyl seats. The man's hair was greased and slicked back to a point behind his head, in the style of ten years ago. At the instant this man had taken his son by the scruff of the neck and thrown him to the floor of the car, his eyes reminded her of Buddy's eyes. She had stood shocked and didn't cross the street until the car had squealed around the corner and disappeared. She never told anyone of this incident. It would have meant siding with Mother and Chrissy against her sister. Every thought and action seemed to be on one side or the other.

Marcia waited for Sharon to finish her hair. She wanted to cry out, "Please don't leave me! Oh, don't just go off with him and leave me all alone!" but these words sat inside her unmoving, as if a stone had settled on them.

Sharon appeared at breakfast in rollers and face cream. Mother made no comment, except for an abnormally cheerful "Good morning!" Then when she had placed a plate of scrambled eggs and toast in front of Sharon, she knelt down and fished a box out of the cabinet beneath the linen drawer. She handed it quickly to Sharon and withdrew to the sink. "From me," she said. "I mean it's a wedding present from me." But she had startled Sharon so that the box had landed lightly on top of Sharon's toast. Sharon continued chewing slowly and wiped the butter and jelly carefully from the box with her napkin. Then she opened it. Inside was a cup and saucer, patterned red, pink, and gold. The rim of the cup was scalloped and the handle came to three little points.

"There are eleven more," said Mother, making a great to-do with the soapsuds. "It's Spode. Mr. Van Dam's mother gave them to me on my wedding day twenty years ago. The rest are packed in the hall closet."

"Thank you, Mother," said Sharon turning the cup over in one hand and the saucer in the other. "I mean I just don't know what to say."

"Enjoy them in good health," said Mother and she walked into the living room and began to vacuum furiously.

FOURTEEN

"You called her *Mother*," whispered Marcia. "I've never heard you call her Mother before."

"I guess I'll have to from now on," said Sharon, not taking her eyes off the label that said "Spode—Made in England." "Spode is real expensive stuff . . . old-fashioned but expensive. I never thought she'd do anything like that. Especially since her and Daddy gave us all that silver."

"She's funny," said Marcia. "She's so funny."

Marcia made no mistakes during the wedding service. She had been positive she would trip or forget to lift her sister's veil or laugh or cry. Someone had stenciled the words "Help Help" on the soles of Buddy's shoes, but he had erased this and it was visible only to the people at the altar when he knelt.

After the ceremony the members of the wedding party were packed tightly into a rented Cadillac limousine for the ride to the VFW hall. Although Marcia was drenched in sweat from the hot June sun by the time they reached the reception, she was still excited about riding in such an impressive long, black Cadillac. She had seen such cars around town occasionally, with important-looking people sitting in the back. She admired the red leather seats, the neatly shaved nape of the chauffeur's neck, and the soundlessness of the motor. It was spoiled only slightly by Chrissy's remark that Cadillacs polluted the environment and if she were ever to get married she would insist that everybody ride horses.

Just as Marcia was about to heft herself out of the back seat, John extended his hand and assisted her expertly out of the car to her feet. John was grinning. He was very handsome, even in his ill-fitting white dinner jacket, rented for the occasion of being an usher at Sharon's wedding. He had taken this duty on in good humor. Chrissy did not seem particularly honored to be a bridesmaid. She said she hated wearing dresses, but Mother had poked her and made her do it.

Next to John stood his girl friend, the new one Mother didn't like very much. Her curly brown hair was tied carelessly in a fuzzy knot behind her head, and she was wearing a long brown batik dress with turquoise love beads. Her name was Carla, she announced to Marcia in a firm voice and shook hands with her equally firmly. Her fingers were skinny and brown and her nails were cut off bluntly like a boy's. Carla wore no makeup.

Marcia's lips parted slightly in mute embarrassment. She could think of nothing to say to this strange girl who was trying so hard to be friendly. Briefly it occurred to her that perhaps Carla had sensed the alignments in the family already. Could this self-assured Carla be seeking out an ally because she was on the wrong end of one of Mother's disapproving stares that morning? The notion dissipated as Marcia's attention flagged. Carla spoke of jumbled, grown-up things in a New York City accent, and her intelligence gave her away as another one of "them."

An impatient sweating man with a large square camera herded Marcia and John into the VFW hall and stood them before a shiny green curtain with the rest of the wedding party. Buddy looked flushed and drank his champagne in large gulps, but then he too was made to pose. Clearly Sharon was more interested in the photographs than Buddy. Marcia tried to conceal the sweat pouring down her dress by clamping her arms flat against herself. She wanted desperately not to ruin her sister's wedding pictures; everything must be perfect for Sharon. But the photographing session went on and on and she only made herself hotter by being so nervous. Mother took it all with surprising good spirits. Marcia expected an outburst of some kind about having the wedding at home, things being prettier and cooler in the garden, but Mother said nothing. She's probably so glad to get her married off, and she doesn't really care about Sharon's wedding, anyway, Marcia thought. Buddy kept sneaking drags on friends' cigarettes and sips of champagne from their glasses between popping flash-bulbs. That angered the photographer, who admonished them, like a schoolteacher, that "some people made things harder and longer for others." Sharon saw the look on Mother's face and tried coquettishly to take the champagne glass from Buddy's hand.

"Hey—I got a right, don't I?" he said. "I mean it's my wedding!"

Everyone laughed uneasily.

The photographer finally said he was finished, at least for the moment, and Marcia was seated at the far end of the bridal table between two of Buddy's friends—ushers she did not know—but John trotted up to her side and switched his place-card with the one next to her. "They'll never know," he said chuckling. Marcia worried that someone would get angry with John and there would be a scene. She could not predict John's behavior, but he did seem to have little respect for the wedding and might spoil Sharon's day by messing up the seating arrange-ments. Still, it was a little exciting that John just took the law into his own hands and did what pleased him. She found it hard to believe that he wanted to sit next to her. Had he been fighting with Mother? John felt sorry for her, she decided.

Bouquets of pink daisies and purple carnations were set symmetrically down the length of the table, just as Sharon had ordered. John picked out a daisy and looked at it closely. "Jesus Christ!" he said and shook his head. Marcia jumped a little. What could be wrong now? As far as she could tell, every-thing was perfect. The flowers went with Sharon's bridal scheme exactly. "How could anybody dye a flower?" John asked.

Marcia did not know. It had not occurred to her that the flowers had been dyed. She shut her mind against John's remarks and Mother's piercing looks and sought out her father's face at the other end of the table, but, as usual, it was as expressionless as a melon.

Suddenly Sharon rose from her seat to see what was going on in the back of the hall. Buddy jumped to his feet as if he had been expecting a disturbance and was accustomed to dealing with them. His mouth tightened as he made his way around the table, whispering, "Just a minute, just a minute." Something would spoil it for Sharon, Marcia thought, and they'd all say "I told you so" afterward. But she could not see past the pillars to the back of the hall. The trouble had apparently transferred itself outside. There a screeching of tires ended it, but Marcia understood a terrible fragility in her sister. All Sharon's usual determined substance melted away as she half-stood at the table with her eyes riveted to a spot of blood on Buddy's lower lip.

The band remembered itself at this moment and broke into the melody from the Pepsi-Cola jingle.

Marcia did not catch the bridal bouquet, despite its being hurled into the air three or four times for the benefit of the photographer. Sharon's best friend, Francine, managed to catch it every time it was thrown. Marcia didn't really believe Francine was destined to marry next because of this, but she knew it was important to Francine to catch it and Sharon had promised to try and throw it to her. Francine was pleased and blushed at the hoots and catcalls directed toward her boyfriend Freddy. Freddy made no attempt to catch the garter. The garter was also thrown three or four times and each time Buddy's friends jumped for it like basketball players. The boy who finally took possession of it wore it around his head like an Indian until he passed out on three folding chairs in an anteroom.

Marcia stood behind Carla and John during all the throwing. Neither of them participated. When Francine caught the bouquet for the last time, Carla turned and said, "Don't worry, you're much prettier anyway!" Marcia could not explain. She had *let* Francine catch it. It was very important to Francine. "I don't know why they can't just do it once," Carla went on. "It ruins the whole thing to let a photographer run a wedding."

"But Sharon wouldn't have a picture for her wedding album otherwise," Marcia said.

Carla did not answer this. John nudged her and sighed. "It's like everything else," he said. "The President doesn't even throw out the first ball of the season right anymore. He tosses out about three for the photographers and then they don't even use them in the game. They just give them back to him."

The red Camaro was covered with shaving cream and crepe-paper streamers. Marcia could hardly see around the crowd as her sister and Buddy ran through showers of confetti to the car. She was not able to throw even one handful, although she had it ready in her clenched fist. Someone threw rice. Rice had been specifically forbidden by the VFW hall because it supposedly attracted mice.

The Rapid Shave words slid down the sides of the car in the heat. A firecracker went off as Buddy pressed the starter and lurched into gear. Marcia saw only the red tail of the car vanish into the traffic, laden with tin cans.

"Well, I guess that's that," said Mother, removing her hat. Then she added, "I think some of Sharon's friends brought their own liquor."

There were indeed quite a number of Old Mr. Boston bottles standing empty near a trash can.

"They aren't Sharon's friends—they're Buddy's friends," said Marcia loyally.

"Well, they're Sharon's friends now," said Chrissy.

But John laughed and needled his mother. "What the hell do you expect?" he said. "You give everybody *one* glass of champagne. Don't be such a prude, you'd think they were shooting smack!"

Marcia let the globs of bleeding confetti fall from her hand as they waited for her father to bring the car around to the front of the hall.

Marcia locked the door to her room and pulled the shades over the late afternoon glare. Gratefully she removed a Milky Way bar and a new movie magazine from her top drawer. She had saved these treats against her sister's leaving and had looked forward to them all day. She felt pleasantly self-sufficient.

The cover of the magazine promised to tell all about David Cassidy's love life, his one real heartbreak, and the one thing he could never tell the girl he marries. It did not bother Marcia that whoever that girl might someday be could quite easily pick up this magazine and read for herself. She knew the stories inside would not live up to the headlines on the cover, but she still could not resist buying magazines about David. Last month's issue had promised to tell everything about the girl David would marry. Marcia had read the article fearfully, but it only listed such qualities as originality, sense of humor, and character that David would one day look for in a wife. They had done it just to scare her. Marcia made mental notes of the qualities, however. Surely she couldn't be said to have much of a sense of humor, because she never made people laugh, and she had never been told she was original. Character she doubted she had. It sounded very much like "personality," which she knew for a fact she lacked. Sue Sturgiss had personality. She was the most popular girl in the class. Still, the last quality listed was devotion. David's wife would have to really really love him and the children they would have. That Marcia felt capable of doing. Perhaps one day, by accident, she would meet him and he would not yet have found a girl who really really loved him. There would be no problem.

Marcia first read all the articles in the magazine about the Osmond Brothers, the Jackson Five, and Ethel Kennedy and saved the David ones the way she saved the middle of her Milky Way bar. She knew better than to expect much about his love life and found out only that with his busy singing schedule he didn't have the time for a love life, but if he had, he would have liked it to be with the girl next door. "Just Like YOU!" the magazine promised. The one thing he could never tell the girl he married was the word good-bye, because there was too much divorce around these days anyway and it was bad for marriage, he had apparently observed to the exclusive interviewer.

Marcia saved the heartbreak article for after dinner and sat back contentedly. She removed the new David centerfold poster to put up on her bulletin board with the others. Then she flipped the radio on and began to sing softly with it.

> You're talking to a dreamer,
> Can't you tell?

She thought about meeting David. She would wait until he gave a concert in Boston. She would save her money and buy beautiful casual clothes, and then she'd go down to the Boston Garden and walk around until she saw him at the stage door. Then she'd ask for directions, just as if she didn't know who he was. That would set her apart from all the screaming teen-agers who wanted pieces of his clothing. David would be intrigued if she didn't recognize him. David, with his long shining hair and his white-and-silver outfits showing just a little bit of chest fuzz. They used to retouch that out of the magazine photos with flesh-colored paint; Marcia could tell. But now they left it in.

Marcia sat wide-eyed, tugged along by her daydreams, no longer listening to the radio. The dream ended the same way every time. She put off the ending as long as she could to savor the details of their wedding. They would be married on a hilltop in California, with only a few friends and family in attendance. Marcia wore her grandmother's eggshell wedding dress in the dream and carried real orange blossoms. She added Mother's face and Chrissy's face this time, consumed in jealousy as David lifted her veil to kiss her. That was the end, but David kissing her always caused her head to feel so light that she thought it might spin around the room of its own accord. When she pictured it at night—after Sharon was asleep— she frightened herself with a dark pounding that began between her eyes with the thought and caused her to be powerless not to touch herself. Marcia knew this was wrong but she did it again and again anyway.

Someone knocked on her door. Marcia stuffed the magazine under the pillow as if it might reveal some secret.

"Mom says . . . I mean, well, I wondered if you wanted to come down to Bailey's with me and maybe take a ride." It was Chrissy, standing in the doorway in a plaid shirt and blue jeans. Mr. Bailey's daughters were in college, but their pony was still home. Chrissy mucked out his stall and groomed him for the privilege of riding him every day after school. Chrissy had more than once described the pony as zippy. The idea of riding anything made Marcia's stomach quail.

"Ride?" she asked in disbelief. Instantly Chrissy looked embarrassed. She's trying to make up for that remark about Buddy's friends, Marcia guessed. She's trying to be nice. For that reason Marcia said yes instead of no.

Marcia put on a pair of Sharon's purple bell-bottoms, because she had no dungarees, and her stacked-heel white vinyl boots. Chrissy's face was almost approving, although normally, Marcia suspected, she would have had a very strong reaction to this outfit.

The stable behind Mr. Bailey's house was a dusty single stall made over from a garage. Morris, the pony, munched on bits of straw, his head hanging over the half-door as he waited for Chrissy to come and take him out. Chrissy put a lump of sugar in Marcia's hand.

"Now just hold your palm out flat like this, fingers together, and let him take it right off your hand," she explained. "He can't hurt you if you hold your hand flat."

Marcia had not planned on going anywhere near the horse's mouth. She had hoped she could have gotten away just by accompanying Chrissy and watching her. She reached up trembling and shrieked when she saw Morris's big yellow teeth. Morris was not prepared for a shriek. He bucked and kicked the sides of his stall with a sound like a shotgun going off.

"Try it again. Let him get to know you," Chrissy said, as if nothing had happened. But Marcia backed away. To her horror, Chrissy opened the stall door. She reached for Morris's halter and stroked him gently on the neck, all the time making little cooing noises as if she were talking to a baby. Marcia watched from a safe distance. Then Chrissy slipped a bridle over his head, led him out into the yard, and with one quick jump was seated astride his bare back.

"Now I won't get him too excited, I'll just calm him down for you," Chrissy announced and she took several speedy turns around the ring. "Then you can use the saddle—somewhere there's a saddle," she said hopefully.

After about fifteen minutes of searching, Chrissy came up with a dusty English saddle missing one stirrup. As she fastened the girth she explained to Marcia about saddle blankets and saddle sores. Marcia waited on an overturned wooden tub. Finally she eased herself onto the pony's back. She sat petrified, holding the reins like airplane throttles until Chrissy told her how to position her hands on the pony's withers and how to keep her heels down and grip with her knees. Marcia could only pray that this space of time would soon be over. Why anybody would voluntarily get up on one of these animals was something she could not understand. "Remember," Chrissy said, as she took the lead line. "He's much bigger than you, but you're much smarter than him, so you have the advantage." That did not sound like much of an advantage to Marcia. Besides, Morris looked unconscionably cunning.

Chrissy jogged next to the pony until she was tired, then she told Marcia to take him around once herself. Marcia managed to make two circuits of the ring, one at a walk and one at a trot that the pony himself started without her urging. She figured he would try a gallop the next time and clear the fence with no trouble.

"Stop!" she commanded him.

"Say 'Whoa!' " said Chrissy, and before Morris could decide what to do about Marcia, she grabbed his bridle and held him while Marcia slipped off.

"You were terrific!" Chrissy said. "Always remember to get off the left-hand side though."

Marcia sat on the washtub and watched Chrissy ride. She was perfectly willing to do this as long as she herself was not asked to get on him again. She pictured telling Lynn the next day that she had been on a horse. No, she wouldn't tell Lynn. Lynn would think she was crazy, but she found herself almost enjoying the afternoon. She nearly felt a part of this strange new family for the first time. She recalled the sensation of Chrissy's hands, fumbling and turning her hands over, pushing her legs forward with a slightly embarrassed laugh. Why did people laugh or look away when they touched each other? It occurred to Marcia, as she watched Chrissy cantering, "equitating" as Chrissy called it, in endless circles, that she had not touched or been touched by anyone, except inadvertently, in several years. All things—her mother's death, her sister's wedding—had passed by without a murmur, like events in someone else's smoothly recounted dream.

She looked down at Sharon's purple pants. The insides of the thighs were covered with fine horsehair and dust. A surge of disloyalty shuddered through her, and she tried to push away the picture of absent Sharon and her inevitable criticisms of whatever Chrissy did.

Chrissy enveloped Marcia with details of horses and riding as they cut across people's backyards on the way home. Marcia listened politely and tried to remember the words. Tack, changing leads, martingale . . . she wondered if a martingale was some sort of bird. Her science teacher had mentioned birds that hung around hippopotamuses and ate the insects off their backs. She decided not to ask Chrissy if this was the case with martingales. Try as she might, Marcia could not scale a waist-high anchor fence and so she walked around it the long way. Chrissy patiently followed her although Marcia had seen her leap over much higher things before.

Chrissy did not seem to be in any hurry, but she did say, "I think it must be after six. Mother'll kill us if we're late."

"I guess she will," said Marcia warily.

"She's awfully sticky, sometimes," Chrissy went on. "It was much worse after Daddy died." She scuffed at a pile of leaves self-consciously.

"Well, she does get mad sometimes," Marcia allowed.

"Mad!" Marcia gave Chrissy a look of desperation when she said this, but Chrissy went on. "When Daddy was alive, she . . . well, Daddy never got mad. He was sort of like your father in that way. Is Mom anything like your mother . . . was?"

"No," Marcia said. "Not at all."

"Do you still miss her very much?"

"Oh, I don't know. Sometimes. Sometimes I just miss our old house and New Bedford."

"I miss Daddy," Chrissy said. "All the time. Sometimes when Mom fights with your father . . . I don't know. She used to fight with Daddy too in just the same way. About other things, though."

"What?"

"Money."

"My father and mother never used to fight."

Chrissy changed the subject slightly. "Did you cry a whole lot when she died?"

"No. Well, everybody said when she died it was a relief. I don't mean that. I mean it took a long time and everybody knew it was coming."

Chrissy bit her lip. "You should have seen Mom," she said. "She cried the whole of a week without stopping and then every night for a year or so—maybe even two years, until she started going out with your father, in fact. I used to hear her. It scared me, even with Johnny home. I wanted to scream at her to stop. One time I went in there in the middle of the night and she looked at me as if she didn't know me. That really scared me. Your father must have done something for her though, because when she started going out with him and all, she stopped crying. When she told me . . . when she told us she was going to get married again to your father, at first I said no and everything, and that I'd run away from home, but now I think it's a good thing. I mean if you think she's bad now, you should have seen her during that . . . time. And now that . . . well now that your sister's married and everything, I think Mom's going to be better. She'll stop being so nervous and picking on you all the time."

Marcia was confused. Was Chrissy saying something nice? Or something not so nice? She decided she wouldn't talk about her father's feelings when her mother had died. She told Chrissy only that she'd been sent down to visit her Aunt Jane in Florida for six weeks after it happened.

"Neat!" said Chrissy.

"Have you ever been to Florida?" Marcia asked cautiously.

"Nope."

"I went on a plane."

"Far out!"

"I guess I've been on a plane about half a dozen times or so," said Marcia casually.

"I've never been in one even once."

"It's fun. It's just like . . . well, flying! Over everything. I mean you can look out the window and see all the fields and cities and roads and when you go through clouds it's like big things of cotton sticking right out there in the air. I'm going to be a stewardess when I grow up." Marcia had not thought about this before. It was nice thinking something definite.

"I'm going to be a vet," said Chrissy.

"A vet," said Marcia evenly.

"A veterinarian, an animal doctor."

"Oh. Well, you'll probably be a good one. How come not a nurse though if you like medicine and stuff?"

"A nurse!"

"Yeah! You get to meet all the cute doctors like on 'Doctor Kildare.' "

"I hate doctors," said Chrissy. "All they do is stick needles in you and nurses just empty icky bedpans."

Marcia had to agree with that.

Mother was beaming at them through the screen door as they turned the corner of the driveway. To Marcia's amazement she continued to beam all through dinner. "How was the ride?" she wanted to know.

"Okay. I mean I didn't fall off, but I almost got bit," said Marcia.

"Bitten. Well, you look none the worse for wear. I should get Chrissy to take me some time. I haven't been on a horse in twenty years or so but it's a terrific way to lose weight."

Marcia was not sure if that remark was directed at her or if Mother was laughing at herself. Mother didn't laugh at herself much, but then she was in an exceptional mood. She had made a steak for dinner. Was she that happy to see Sharon go? Chrissy was full of stories about how well Marcia had done; how she had trotted the first time she'd been on a horse and how she, Chrissy, hadn't done that until at least the fifth time. They were trying. They were trying so hard. Marcia relaxed a little and the hurt of Sharon's leaving began to subside.

Had Marcia known how pretty she looked that morning? That she was the prettiest of all the attendants? Marcia said thank you and noticed that Chrissy, who had been a bridesmaid, seemed delighted at this remark. Was she excited about starting high school in the fall? Yes, she was excited. Mother said they would have to go out and buy new clothes for the girls for the coming school year. She suggested Marcia go to Jordan Marsh with Lynn and buy what she wanted. Marcia didn't believe her ears, but Mother had said this and was looking right at her. She wanted to know—and Marcia in her

astonishment about the trip to Jordan Marsh only heard the
second part of the question—if Sharon had really liked the
china. "Some people," Mother said, "only like modern china."
"Yes," said Marcia. "She liked it fine. She told me so."
"What did she say?"
"She . . . she said she'd heard of . . . whatever the name
was I . . . "
"Spode."
"Spode. And that it was . . . that she was real pleased. I
mean I forget exactly what she said but I know she liked it."

Marcia spent the evening reading a Nancy Drew mystery
since her father wanted to watch baseball on television. Mother
knitted, her legs curled up beneath her comfortably on the
sofa. She made observations about this and that from time
to time which annoyed Chrissy, who was reading something
much fatter than a Nancy Drew, but Marcia didn't really
mind. Her pleasure lasted through the excitement of *The
Clue of the Broken Locket* and the last of the wedding cake
shared by the whole family before bed, but when she switched
on the light in her bedroom, she discovered with a little leap
of her heart that Sharon's bed had been removed from the
room.

· II ·

Marcia inspected herself in the stained girl's-room mirror.
She combed her hair thoughtfully. She and her friends would
be late for English again and Mr. Kovaks would get angry,
but Marcia managed to lose herself among the other girls and
inevitably his anger would be directed at the louder members
of the group—Lynn in particular. Lynn's vixenish little chin
and feral eyes that always darted around the person she was
talking to aggravated the teachers. Marcia had learned long

ago to be polite, to say nothing, and to look as if she hadn't known she'd done wrong. Teachers, she thought, were so anxious to pound their lists of facts into your head. When they got a response from her, a right answer, they were delighted. Marcia never spoke to her teachers unless she had a right answer. Then they smiled and softened a bit—enough, anyway, to give her C's. Most of the other kids in the General Course were trouble. If you stayed out of trouble, they gave you C's.

Marcia toyed with the ends of her hair. She thought about becoming a stewardess. Stewardesses led exciting lives. She had read several articles about them. She would have to make herself beautiful. She would have to lose some weight, but that could be put off for a few years. She pictured a little blue cap with gold wings, pinned to her hair. She would have an apartment in a big city, shared with two other girls, and anytime, even in the middle of the night, she could be summoned to the airport and fly away to sparkling cities in a big, clean plane. The stewardesses she had seen on her six flights were so thin and lovely, and she noticed how they went right up to the cockpit and talked to the pilot, easily, jokingly. Marcia wondered if it would ever be second nature for her to laugh with a man, a wonderful, sinewy, handsome man like those pilots and copilots with their black uniform jackets off and their dark-blue shirt sleeves rolled up. Stewardesses controlled hundreds of people at once. They might look as if they were only fetching drinks and serving dinner, but when they announced on the intercom that the plane was going through turbulence and that everyone must fasten their seat belts, everyone obeyed like children in a class. If you were a stewardess, anything could happen.

"Why don't you get it tipped?" Lynn asked, balancing herself on the sink next to Marcia.

"If I had it tipped she'd kill me," said Marcia.

"What do you care what she thinks? She's not your real mother. She's trying to keep you from being prettier than that scaggy Chrissy."

"There'd be another fight," Marcia said.

"I bet if your sister was home you'd have it tipped." Lynn giggled. "Boy, if I had blond hair like yours I'd have it tipped. I wouldn't stand for her pushing me around."

"Oh, you've got your mother too," said Marcia. "Let's go. We're gonna be late."

"That's new? What do you care? Kovaks, he never even sees you. It's me that gets it all the time." Lynn tried to slam the girls'-room door, but it swung through its arc without a sound.

No, Marcia thought. He doesn't even see me.

Marcia took a *Sixteen* magazine out of her locker and hid it inside her notebook to read during class. She no longer could keep the magazines at home, because Mother threw them out during housecleanings. Lynn was right, too, in her sly little way of knowing things, about Sharon and having her hair tipped. Everything had changed since Sharon had left and Marcia was more alone than she'd thought she'd be. Her father gave her more money now—that was something. But Marcia needed Sharon's presence at dinner. During difficult moments her father's quietness was shadowy and reticent, unlike Sharon's kind of silence, which was as malevolent as a cocked trigger.

Mr. Kovaks called on her. Marcia stood and read a paragraph from the condensed *Merchant of Venice* in their textbook. She pronounced Portia "Por-*shee*-a."

"No," said Mr. Kovaks. "It's Portia, as in Marcia." He grinned at her—hoping she'd be pleased?

"Portia," Marcia continued. She read the words in front of her dutifully. They meant nothing to her. There was a drawing of this Portia at the beginning of the story. She looked like a model, nothing like Marcia. Marcia sat down feeling stupid when she had finished. Mr. Kovaks would not go away.

"I don't think you're thinking about what you're reading, Marcia," he said. "If you had been, you'd have known how to pronounce Portia's name. You couldn't have missed it. It's spelled almost like yours."

Marcia said nothing, hoping he would be satisfied with his lecture and move on to someone in the next row.

"Who is Portia, Marcia? What is the author trying to tell us in *The Merchant of Venice?* What is the story about?"

"It's a book by William Shakespeare," Marcia answered. Why was he attacking her with these questions? She finished her homework and read without stumbling, which was more than the other kids did. She did what was asked of her.

"Doesn't this story mean anything to you, Marcia?"

"Other kids pronounced the name that way," Marcia said.

"Maybe other kids are wrong. Maybe you know better because it's practically your own name. Would you start calling yourself 'Mar-*shee*-a' just because other kids said it that way?"

Marcia blushed at his playing games with her name. "No, I guess not," she said.

"Then why didn't you pronounce it properly when you saw it in a book?"

"I don't know, Mr. Kovaks." Why was he picking on her like this? Why couldn't he go away with his books and his questions? They seemed to mean so much to him—this fat little man with his three gray suits and his one flecked sports jacket.

"Please see me when class is over."

A note was passed to Marcia from Lynn, who sat three seats in back of her. "Tell him where he can put it!" said the note. Marcia crumpled it up. She dared not look back at Lynn. Lynn said things like this all the time, so had Sharon. Marcia was not vulgar. She didn't swear or refer to parts of people's bodies—she was good. Why did everyone press her so?

"I've been noticing you, Marcia," Mr. Kovaks began. Marcia froze. She wished he would have been angry instead of friendly. She wanted him to give her double homework, or send her to detention, or give her a lecture so that she could sit and listen to it and look sorry when it was over. People who got angry didn't expect you to say much afterward. They thought you were crushed, and when their anger was spent, they felt a little badly and wanted to be rid of you. Marcia was never crushed by lectures. That was her secret. She could think of nothing to say about his noticing her. Mr. Kovaks looked tired. She saw that he had dandruff on his lapels.

"I know, and I think you know, Marcia, that of all the people in this class, you can do better." He waited again for a response. Marcia stared at the books in her lap. She didn't want to look at Mr. Kovaks and his nervous hands . . . his lapels.

"You're a bright girl, Marcia. You've got brains. You don't have to stay in this General Course. You could be in College Prep if you wanted."

"I'm not good enough for that," said Marcia confidently.

"Christina Van Dam is your sister, is she not?"

"Well, she's my stepsister, I guess."

"Christina does very well in school. Does that, by any chance, make you hang back? Does it make you not even want to try?"

"No. She's just . . . Chrissy's just smart. I guess I'm not too smart." How could he find his way to the center of her like this? Now that he was there, inching in with his questions, would he stop?

"If I were to ask that you be transferred to my College Prep class, would you give it a try?"

"I don't know."

"You do your homework, Marcia. You do it well. Would you do your homework for a College Prep course?"

"I don't know. I . . . well, I have to do my homework."

"Do you know why I'm suggesting this, Marcia?"

Marcia looked down at her books again. She had written DAVID in large letters on her notebook. "No," she answered.

"Because I think you're bored. For instance, you know perfectly well that *The Merchant of Venice* is a play not a book, even if it is written as a book instead of a play in our textbook. Tell me you're not bored, Marcia."

"No, I'm not bored."

"Marcia, don't be afraid of me. We've been reading that damn thing for two months, excuse my French. Two months of singsong reading aloud is boring. It bores *me!* Wouldn't you like to read more things, more interesting things? Be with the brightest kids in the school? Tell me you're bored!"

Marcia's thoughts fluttered. What answer did this man, with his face three inches from hers, want? Apparently he wanted her to say that she was bored. That would get her into a hard class. But it was true she was bored. She started to giggle. This funny teacher had reached right inside her and now he wanted the truth. They both began to laugh. She was bored, he'd got that much, but she wouldn't add that she thought a harder class would be even more boring. Marcia was laughing with a teacher, a man, like the stewardesses with their pilot, but this man was not tall and wonderful. He was stumpy and tired like her father. "What did she want to be when she grew up?" he wanted to know.

"A veterinarian," Marcia answered. He looked puzzled. "Or maybe a teacher," she added. He brightened.

Marcia and Lynn ate raspberry Good Humors on the way home from school.

"Why did you do it? Why did you say yes?" Lynn whined at her.

"I didn't say yes. He made me."

"Soon you'll be out of all our classes. Soon they'll have you in College Prep history and French and everything. Then you'll have so much homework you'll never be able to have any fun with the kids."

"What could I do?"

"Well, you're not going to go to college, are you?"

Marcia considered. She wanted to go to stewardess school right after high school. Maybe stewardess schools required College Prep. She didn't know. "What could I do about it anyway?" she said. "He thinks I'm some kind of genius or something. Now I'm going to have to read poems and all those long books Chrissy reads. Talk about boring!"

"Well, you ought to stand up for your rights. It's a free country. Tell him tomorrow you've changed your mind."

"I can't. If Mother ever found out it'd be the end of me. Even Daddy's going to like this. He wants me to be as good as Chrissy."

"I never had any friends who weren't in my classes," Lynn said.

"Well, I can't help it, Lynn! Are you going to not be my friend? Is that what you're saying? Just because of stupid old Kovaks?"

"I never said that."

The roof of Marcia's mouth began to ache. She fixed her mind on the inside of a huge clean airplane. Someday this will all be over, she thought, and maybe I'll be on an over-night flight to California. Maybe I'll fly to Mexico and Japan in my slender blue uniform . . . *my* uniform. She refocused on Lynn, who was zigzagging down the path next to her, now talking about how stuck-up all the kids in College Prep were.

Marcia realized that she didn't care if they were stuck-up. Lynn was leaving anyway because Marcia had crossed some line without even meaning to.

"Bye, Portia!" said Lynn, skipping between two cars.

There was a letter from Sharon on the kitchen table when Marcia got home.

"What does it say?" Mother asked before Marcia had a chance to open it.

"I don't know. I'll read it later."

"I thought maybe you'd gone riding again with Chrissy."

Marcia was surprised. The first and only ride had been seven months ago. Mother chopped onions with her usual intensity. She turned her head and covered her eyes with a dish towel. "Ooooh, onions," she gasped and laughed nervously. Marcia opened the refrigerator door and looked for a soda. There was never any there.

"I had to stay after," she said, pouring herself a glass of milk.

"Have a cookie. Why did you have to stay after school?"

Marcia took an oatmeal cookie out of the cannister. She had a Drakes cupcake in her pocketbook but would save it for upstairs. "Oh, Mr. Kovaks," she answered.

"Why did Mr. Kovaks want to speak to you?"

"He wants me to go in another class."

"Oh?"

"Yeah. College Prep. Just for a while." The corners of Marcia's mouth twitched upward as she said this, despite herself.

"Marcia, that's terrific! I'm so proud of you. Wait till your father hears this! Will you be in Chrissy's class?"

"I don't know. I haven't even decided to do it yet."

"Are you happy, Marcia?"

"I don't know."

"Well, it means that Mr. Kovaks thinks you're a lot smarter than we . . . than you thought you were. It sounds to me as if he thinks you're college material."

"No. He doesn't think that." Marcia pictured bolts of material slowly feeding into a wringer. "I'm not going to college," she said. "Maybe if I was a boy, I'd have to, like Daddy went to college but his sister didn't go and Sharon didn't."

"Times have changed, Marcia, you know that. I'm no woman's libber like Chrissy, but I went to college and Chrissy will certainly go. Even if you don't plan on a career afterward, you owe it to your husband and children to have a college education."

"I'm not smart enough."

Mother removed the wax-paper bag of innards from the chicken in front of her. "You know, Marcia," she said, "I think you are. You just never learned to believe in yourself. Maybe your mamma didn't think things like college were important. She may . . . well, she may have had other things on her mind. Or maybe if she'd lived she'd have encouraged you now. You're not a carbon copy of your sister Sharon. It's all well and good for Sharon to have a teen-age marriage, but I wonder if you want that for yourself?"

"What?"

Mother smiled almost mischievously as she piled the onions into the open chicken cavity. "I'm going to ask you please not to say 'what.' What I mean is, that statistically speaking, girls who don't go on to college tend to marry young. Look at Sharon. Now Buddy is in the navy and probably off to Vietnam. Sharon's going to be all alone. Would that make you happy?"

Marcia was lost. She stared at the chicken and tried to picture it with a head and feathers, but she couldn't tell which was the top and which the tail. "They're all going into the service now. That's not Sharon's fault," she said.

"That's not what I said, Marcia. I'll find you the article in *Psychology Today*. Statistics prove that young marriages have a greater divorce rate and unhappiness rate than the more mature marriages."

"Are you telling me my sister is going to be divorced?"

"Marcia, I'm asking you what you want to do with your life. What your goals are. Of course you want to get married. And I think it's fine that Sharon got married. But Sharon is Sharon and you are Marcia. You have a choice available to you and the first door was opened today. By all means seize the opportunity and start believing in yourself. I *know* you can do it."

Marcia closed her eyes against an impending headache. Explaining about Mr. Kovaks's dandruff and Lynn's nastiness was too complicated. She supposed Chrissy believed in herself, but Chrissy was so dumb sometimes, particularly about clothes and boys. Of course Chrissy pretended not to care, but Marcia had seen her, out of the corner of her eye, wistfully looking on as Marcia set her long blond hair or fixed herself in front of the mirror. Once Chrissy had worn a sweater inside-out to school. Marcia had told her about it just before the bus came, and Chrissy had shamefacedly walked back to the house to put it right. Marcia felt sorry. She hadn't intended to humiliate her.

"Are you listening, Marcia?"

"I have a headache. Maybe I'll lay down."

"Lie, not lay. You wouldn't get headaches if you took vitamin B. Just look it up in Adele Davis. How would you like to try a full College Prep course next term, not just English? Just to try it, of course."

Vitamins and headaches blurred in Marcia's thoughts. The books and articles Mother was always talking about—the surveys and the continuous flow of information into and out of her—Mother believed in so many things, the way Lynn's mother believed in her saints' pictures and rosary beads strung all around her bedroom. Lynn laughed at the medals and dried palm fronds. Marcia decided it was not so easy to laugh at vitamins and statistics. Mother was not letting her go. There was something she was supposed to say here. "I'll try," she answered seriously.

"You mean a full College Prep course, not just English?"

How had this happened? The right answer five minutes ago was now not enough. "I'll ask Daddy," said Marcia.

"Marcia, be your*self!*"

"Be myself?"

"Don't be someone else's idea of yourself. There's a whole world of wonders out there for you. If you shrink from it, you'll be sorry when it's too late."

Marcia enjoyed her Drakes cake slowly. She folded the wrapper into a tiny square and put it back in her pocketbook. Mother would be sure to find it in the wastepaper basket if she tried to throw it out. She opened Sharon's letter.

Dear Sis,

Greetings from the resort city of Pennsecola, Fla. (ha ha) Seriously life on the base isnt too bad but some of the people are far out. One girl here whose husband is in the Nam is real neat. She comes from Portland Maine but so far she is the only one from our neck of the woods. She doesn't expect him to come back she says because if she thinks that then she'll worry all the time and so she acts like she isnt married at all. Except she doesn't mess around if that's what you think. Buddy is gone all nights except on weekends so what do you think of that for married life? Someday remind me to tell you all the gorry details (ha ha) ! ! ! ! !

It looks like he's going to go in another month after basic is finished. All the girls here just hang around and talk about the Nam and it's depressing. Some say they don't like the war but most are very patriotic and like Nixon and think we should beat the commies. But they don't like hippies or people talking out against the war. Everyone wants it just to be over and the boys to come home with victory and not shame. Some of the girls here mess around with the recrutes if their husbands have been gone long enough. But I would never do that and neither would my friend Denise (from Portland.) We are in housing now but Buddy says he wants to buy a mobil home in Tropic Paradise off base before he leaves so we might although Daddy'd have to help us with the money. What I don't want is to get pregnent now although I had a scare last month but it wasn't true (Thank God) ! ! ! ! ! Thank god for Daddy too because even though Buddy has settled down I know he's there and you are there too and sometimes I hate the base like poisin and feel like I'm in the navy too. There is a contingent of Waves here and you should see them. We are still hoping for the Meditaranian but the odds are ten to one against so don't hope too much. Still they say most of the jobs in the Nam are desk jobs and it isn't as bad as Korea was. Maybe I'll go see Aunty Jane when Buddy leaves. Spend a few days there— although I never could stand her. Maybe you could come down for Xmas vacation.

It sure is lonely. Maybe I'll get a cat. There's stacks

of stray cats around here. I miss you and Daddy.
Don't forget to write. Bye Now.

Love,
Shar

Marcia read the letter three times. She heard Chrissy bang
the kitchen door downstairs and Mother tell her not to bang
the door. Chrissy groaned hideously and Marcia knew Mother
must have told her to brush her hair or wash her face. It was
curious how nobody ever seemed exactly right for anybody
else's taste. If she had Chrissy's brains, she would be close to
perfect because she took personal grooming habits seriously.
If Chrissy were neater, she too would be near perfect. As things
were, Chrissy was more perfect than Marcia, however. She
wanted to think about Sharon, but she could only think of
how to explain this letter to Mother, who seemed inordinately
interested in it, and to her father, who would be upset by it.
Her father would want Sharon home again and Mother would
not and there would be fights. She began to imagine them,
Mother buzzing around her father's chair with all her reasons
so solidly figured out, so organized, and so endless. Her father
would say absolutely nothing until Mother was finished. Then
he would restate whatever he'd made up his mind to do in
the first place and that would set Mother off all over again.
Marcia suspected that there had been an agreement between
them, although it had never been mentioned, that Sharon must
not live here.

Chrissy came in without knocking. "Hey! Did you get a
letter from your sister? Is Buddy gone yet?"

"No, maybe another month or so."

"Oh. Can I read it?"

Marcia wavered for an instant. She saw no reason to make
an issue of it. "Sure," she said.

Chrissy held the letter in one hand while she undressed herself with the other. Marcia couldn't help thinking that whatever Chrissy did, she was always reading something at the same time. Maybe that was how people got to be like Mother— vast founts of information had to pour out of them to allow space for everything new they crammed in. Chrissy's eyes flickered through the letter. "The spelling isn't too good," said Marcia, as if to explain something. Hearing herself, she felt as if she had suddenly dropped an ice cube down her own back.

Chrissy handed back the letter. "You think she's going to come back here when he goes?"

"I don't know. She doesn't mention it. I don't know."

"Boy, that'd sure do Mom in! I bet you want her back though."

"If she's unhappy. I don't want her to be lonely."

"Mom wouldn't think about that," Chrissy admitted. "Hey, what's this I hear about you getting out of General?"

"Did Mother tell you that?"

Chrissy shrugged again. "No, I just heard," she said.

"I don't know."

"Well, c'mon. Is it true?"

"Maybe. I'll have to ask my father."

"Well, can I say something about your father without being critical or anything?"

"Go ahead."

"Well, I think he's a really terrific guy and all, but I think he has some old-fashioned ideas. About girls. He might tell you to stay where you are and become a secretary or a stew- ardess or something, and I think you're really smart, Marsh. I mean the College Course is no great shakes. It's boring but it isn't that hard and if you took it maybe you could make up your own mind, and not just be automatically destined for a crummy job." Chrissy had run out of words and breath. She stood lamely in the doorway for a minute. She didn't even fill out her underwear—no breasts or hips to speak of and her knees were knobby and her feet too big. To Marcia she looked like an adolescent boy. "I guess I shouldn't have said that," Chrissy added, "about the stewardess, but—"

"What does it matter what people say?" Marcia broke in. "Everyone thinks I'm stupid. Now maybe they don't think I'm all that dumb and they rush around like crazy trying to push me into doing something. Mr. Kovaks is a creep. I should have told him off in the first place like Lynn said to."

"I think he's a creep too. And he has dandruff."

But Marcia couldn't laugh at this. She did not look up at Chrissy.

"Gee, did Mom give you one of her lectures?" Chrissy asked. She had wrapped her clothes into a ball and was tossing them gingerly from hand to hand.

"I'll say she did."

"You've got to understand about Mom. Sometimes she's awful and I can't stand her either but she's usually right."

Marcia looked up. "Aren't you afraid she'll hear you?" she whispered.

"No."

Apparently the thought had never crossed Chrissy's mind.

Marcia sat on the floor with her back resting against her father's knees. She dawdled through her homework, not listening to his hockey game. Mother observed that in the future Marcia would have to concentrate more fully on her homework and not watch television while she did it.

"But I'm not watching. Daddy's watching. I'm just sitting here."

"*Sparky, let her alone*," said Marcia's father in Marcia's imagination. He tamped out his pipe severely in the ashtray and turned to Mother. *"Leave her be! She's not your daughter. Why do you always pick, pick, pick? Never let anything or anyone be until they're just what you want. Never let anything alone until it's like this frigid symmetrical living room with your knickknacks exactly dusted every day and the picture of your first husband catty-corner on the bureau where I don't put out a picture of my first wife. Marcia doesn't hurt anyone. She's a good girl."*

Marcia looked up at her father. He was staring dreamily at the hockey players. She wondered if he had heard Mother's remark, or if he even heard the television. His pipe had gone out. He had said nothing for the last half hour.

"You know that's true though, don't you, Marcia?" Mother continued.

"Know what?"

"That you're going to have more homework and you're going to have to do it at your desk as Chrissy does."

"I guess so."

"Well, then you've decided to make the full switch!"

"I didn't think about it."

"Charles, has Marcia told you about Mr. Kovaks?"

Marcia's father turned slowly. "No, what about Mr. Kovaks?"

"He thinks Marcia should be in the College Preparatory Course instead of the General. He thinks she's way above the others in her class."

"That's nice."

"He didn't say that!" Marcia interrupted. "He just said English and he didn't say anything about the rest of the kids."

"But you do want to do it, don't you?"

"I *said* I'd talk to Daddy about it."

"Well, you're certainly not going to advise her to stay back, are you, Charles?"

Fifteen

"Carla?"

"Yes?"

"How come you go out there to dinner all the time if you hate it so much?"

Carla sniffed in the freezing Boston night. "I don't know," she said. "It's only about every three or four weeks or so. She's always calling. Johnny just can't say no to her, I guess. Well, he does say no. If he didn't we'd be out there every week. He . . . he prefers not to do battle with her and it's easier that way. It's not so bad. She ignores me for the most part and so does Chrissy. I like talking to you, Marsh. It makes it worth it."

Marcia found this hard to believe, but it pleased her tremendously. Why Carla the smart, Carla the independent should enjoy talking to her, Marcia, was a mystery. In the year and a half since she had first met Carla, Carla had practically adopted her. Perhaps it was only because Mother and Chrissy were so mean, so stony and correct to her, and Marcia was the only person she could talk to in the whole family except, of course, for John. John, Marcia had noticed, was just dreadful during visits to his mother's. He never said a thing. He had been nice this weekend though, during Marcia's visit to Boston. He acted as if he were her real older brother, not just a stepbrother. He had been so considerate, picking her up in the car at North Station, taking her the long way to the apartment so that she could see the Haymarket and Fanueil Hall and State Street.

"Carla?" Marcia asked again.

"Yup?"

"Are you and John . . . are you and John going to get married?"

"Mother put you up to that one, didn't she!" Carla said, laughing.

Marcia blushed. "No, no. I just wondered."

"She's still saying the same old stuff about me?"

"Oh, yes. All the time."

"Immoral hippie corrupting her son." Carla trod heavily in the snow as she said the word *son*.

"Something like that," Marcia answered. "Oh, except one more thing. She said she was surprised at your parents because Jewish families usually exercise more control over their children, but nowadays, even the Jews are losing out."

"That's a good one."

"She doesn't talk about happiness statistics the way she does about Sharon, I guess, because you and John aren't married and maybe *Consumer Reports,* or whatever the name of that thing she reads is, doesn't do surveys on that. Does your family give you a lot of grief?"

"God no. They don't mind one bit that I'm living with

Johnny. They love him, and my mother thinks he'll keep the stranglers away. She thinks Boston is full of stranglers. Did I tell you they even brought us up a rotisserie?"

"Boy!"

"I guess I still didn't answer your question. We'll probably get married if and when we decide to have kids. Speaking of married, how's your sister?"

"Okay, I guess. She has a lot of friends on the base and she was glad to be back after all the fighting at home. She says she's going to get a job. Something for the phone company like she did before she was married."

"That sounds nice. Hey . . . did she really start up something with that guy?"

"No. Moose is just an old high-school friend. She just wanted to have a little fun for the evening. I mean for the love of Mike, Buddy's been away almost a year now. But Mother doesn't approve of the Starlight Room, and I guess my sister had something to drink. She said she only had one cocktail, and then she started fooling around, but as far as I know, she only took her shoes off. She didn't do anything. Anyhow, I was asleep the whole time, but Chrissy said she watched them from the landing, down in the living room and she said they did a whole bunch of stuff, and then Mom—Mother went down and saw what was going on and sent Moose home and told Sharon to pack and be out by morning."

"And she did?"

"Yeah, but she told me she only took her shoes off."

"Moose is married, isn't he?"

"Yes, but his wife isn't home hardly at all."

"How about your father?"

"He said he wouldn't kick his own daughter out of the house no matter what she did, and Mother asked him if he approved of what Sharon did. Messing around while Buddy was away, and he said No, but still, and then he said Moose was to blame for getting her drunk and maybe giving her some pot, and that Sharon didn't know what she was doing. By that time my sister had left anyway. She left before Daddy was up."

"Carla?"

"Yup?"

"Do you and John smoke pot?"

"We used to but it makes John paranoid so we don't anymore."

"Mother thinks you do."

"She probably thinks we have orgies in the middle of Harvard Square too."

"No. She just says she wishes you'd get married. Then she says she'd like you."

Carla laughed as if she thought this was a hysterical remark. "We're here," she said, pointing to a theater marquee and taking out her wallet. "This is on me now."

"I have money."

"On John and me. This is our weekend to treat you."

"But I'd like to pay you back. You've paid for dinner and the museum and everything. Daddy gave me fifty dollars before I left and I've only spent six ninety-five so far."

"Okay, I'll let you."

Marcia felt slightly charged with pleasure as she pushed a ten dollar bill through the window to the ticket seller. "Do you think he's cold in there?" she asked.

"He well may be," said Carla thoughtfully.

Marcia thought of Carla as one of "them" simply because she could hold her own with Mother or anyone else who came along. Carla was intelligent and not ashamed of it, and she definitely had her own world. Nevertheless, she always answered Marcia's questions and never acted as if Marcia were stupid—

or even young. "Please don't say anything to Mother or anyone that I went to foreign movies or museums or anything, will you?" she asked suddenly.

"If you want me not to say anything, I won't," said Carla. She didn't ask why. She didn't seem to want to get inside Marcia and pluck something out. Perhaps she knew the answer already.

They sat down in the back of the half-empty theater. Marcia tried as hard as she could to concentrate on the grainy black-and-white movie. She wished it were at least in color. Everything was twice as serious in black and white. The name of the movie was *Quatre Cents Coups.* Carla had said it was a must for anyone who had not seen it. It was a sad movie, she explained, and had made her cry several times. Marcia noticed how quickly Carla's eyes sped through the subtitles and took in their meaning. She hoped Carla would not cry this time but was prepared to ignore it respectfully if she did. The translation of the title made no sense. "The Four Hundred Blows." She had thought about that title all the way to the movie, trying to find some meaning in it. Words from the grown-up world usually hid something. At times, if she thought long enough she could figure out what, but more often than not they were sprung upon her in deadly ambush by teachers, and then dangled before her like a set of keys to doors she couldn't even name. She found it difficult to believe that French was a language people really spoke, like English. The subtitles disappeared too quickly and the meaning of the story was obscured from her.

Carla did not cry. Perhaps she never cried and only said she did. Marcia could not conceive of Carla red-eyed and puffy. She could not even imagine that Carla had ever been a child. No one would dare stick their icy ideas inside of her. Suddenly she was overcome with a desire to put her head in

Carla's lap, but the velvet arm of the theater seat was between them and she dismissed the thought with a little shock, as if she had just been missed by a speeding taxi.

They trudged to the subway in the dirty, sopping snow. Marcia thought about the little boy in the movie; how he had cocked his head and squinted into the sun. He was standing in the ocean in the last frame. "What does 'Four Hundred Blows' mean?" she asked at last.

"I don't know," said Carla. "Maybe it means that's all a person can stand."

Marcia laughed a little bit. "I thought you might think that was a stupid question," she said.

"Of course it isn't a stupid question. If you don't know something, it's stupid *not* to ask."

They said nothing more until they were seated on the subway back to Beacon Hill.

"Why are you so afraid of being called stupid, Marcia?" Carla asked.

"I don't know. I guess everybody thinks I am."

"Who? Who thinks you're stupid? I don't think so. John doesn't think so. Who thinks so?"

"Oh. Carla . . . I don't know. I guess I think so. You know, ever since I started College Prep . . . Well, it's just that even though I'm doing all right, I can't help feeling that I don't belong there . . . that I'm . . . I'm on one of those things, a conveyor belt or something and it keeps going faster and faster, and so far I've kept up, but I'm afraid everything's going to come crashing down on me someday."

"Why?"

"I don't know. Maybe I'm just insecure or something. Math isn't so bad. I do okay in math. I even caught up to Chrissy's class in French, almost. I do okay in everything, as a matter of fact. Somehow I got a B in English. It took a lot of work. I must have studied for . . . it felt like a hundred hours . . . for the exam. Other kids . . . I don't think they have to study so hard. Chrissy . . . Chrissy actually cried at the end of *Romeo and Juliet*. I mean she's always crying over the least thing, but a stupid old play in a book! I mean maybe you don't think it's a stupid old play, I didn't mean that. But Chris, she even writes poetry herself. She . . . God, she even reads the *New York Times*. She does her homework in less than half the time it takes me. She hardly has to study at all."

"Do you always feel compared to Chrissy?"

"Yes, in a way. I mean no one has to say anything. I know what they mean, even the teachers."

"Are you in her classes?"

"One. Latin. College Prep has its own levels and Chrissy's in all the pilot classes. I'm not, of course. Last week we had a test. I studied for four hours. I got a ninety-one. Chrissy didn't study at all and she got a hundred. And then do you know what Mom—Mother said? She said my ninety-one was really better than Chrissy's hundred because I'd come so far so fast or something and Chrissy *agreed* with her."

"Marcia—you—I just don't see how you can take it. Chrissy's like, well, it must be like living with Bobby Fischer."

"Who's Bobby Fischer?"

"He's a chess champion, a real genius, but you have nothing to worry about. If you'd think a little better of yourself, you wouldn't worry so much. And worrying is half the battle. Living a life, in the world, doesn't have anything to do with grades. I mean I suppose you need grades, but it's too bad you can't just skip over all this and be in the world, alive, doing something instead of competing over Shakespeare. It's different, though, once you get to college. It's better. I mean I love my job in the studio now, but I had a lot of fun in college."

"College!"

"I'm serious. What do you think? Just because Chrissy does a little better than you in school now, that that's got anything to do with you or what will happen to you as an adult?"

"I know I'll never go to college. I know that much."

Carla laughed a deep musical laugh. "Someday, if you ever go down to New York, to Bronxville, it's not far, drop in at Sarah Lawrence. You might like the idea. In the meantime don't worry about Chrissy. You know what I think of Christina Van Dam anyway."

"You don't like her."

"No."

"Johnny likes her though."

"What can I tell you? She's his sister. She's not here this weekend though. You are."

"She was angry about that," Marcia said. "She tried not to show it but she was jealous as all get-out. I heard her talking to Mother. The way they talk, you can hear everything in that house."

"Through the walls."

"Through the walls, through the floor, through the roof! Sometimes I even hear things I don't hear. Sometimes I even hear them talking when I'm miles away from the house. That's stupid of course."

Carla sighed. "No," she said, "I've heard things in that house too—about me—when I was in the next room. I know just what you mean."

The train screamed and lurched as it approached the trestle above Cambridge Street. Dirty black water flowed back and forth on the floor. Marcia read and reread a reducing advertisement over the empty seats opposite her. One of her troubles was being overweight. She would have liked to be as thin as Carla or as the girl in the picture. She thought about how it would feel to be thin enough to disappear, at least not to be everyone's fat target all the time.

Marcia did not ask what Carla had heard. Carla had her troubles with Mother, but Carla was able not to care, or at least she said that the things that were important to Mother didn't matter to her. Grades, money, and "what people would think" were things Carla despised. There was a whole world of other things that meant a great deal to Carla. Mother thought them trivial. Marcia admired them from a distance. She read the books Carla gave her, but whether it was Joseph Conrad or Kahlil Gibran, she always felt, upon finishing them, that she had paused beneath the lip of a giant bowl and had been unable to look in. Marcia searched in all of the books for the secret to How You Live, which Carla stressed among all others as The Most Important Thing, but since she had little choice in how she lived, she decided that perhaps it was better not to know.

Carla and John's apartment had only two and a half rooms, but it was packed full of more things than would fit in an entire house. The kitchen wall was hung with beautiful implements—tin grinders and oriental pots and big wooden ladles and straw brushes. Carla used all these things and cooked Chinese and Greek dinners. Marcia never cared much about food, except for desserts, but this was another thing that meant a great deal in Carla's world.

Marcia sat in a beanbag chair that molded itself perfectly to her sprawl and accepted a glass of sherry from John. Two of his law school classmates sat in other beanbags. Carla kissed them both gaily and introduced Marcia.

Jerry kept flicking his longish red curls out of his eyes. Marcia was fascinated. Jerry didn't seem in the least perturbed when she said she was a sophomore in high school. She started talking to her new best friend, Carol Kubiak, in her imagination: *"He was so cute. I mean long red hair and over six feet tall . . . No, we didn't do much . . . Well, maybe you wouldn't call it a date exactly but we did have some drinks together . . . Harvard . . . Yes, I told him I was a sophomore in high school . . . He said I looked old for my age . . . How should I know if I'll see him again, maybe yes, maybe no . . . Well, I wouldn't say I didn't touch him . . . I'm not going to tell you . . . Maybe he did and maybe he didn't . . . Carol, some things are private . . . Well, I didn't exactly slap him in the face . . . No, of course not, above the waist . . . Well, all right, below the neck. . . . No, he didn't, and I wouldn't tell about it if he did!"*

Marcia was having trouble following Jerry's conversation. He hunched forward in his beanbag and told her all about a rent strike. She focused on phrases like "absentee landlord" and "tenants' organization" long enough to nod in the right places and even ask a few questions she hoped were intelligent. The sherry stirred a sweet confidence in her that she could not remember feeling ever before. "Who is the leader of the tenants' organization?" she asked, staring at the seam under his fly.

"Well, that's the guy I was telling you about," said Jerry. "Nathan. And his wife, she's a fantastic lawyer and the board doesn't know it yet but they're going to win. It's going to be a precedent for the whole country."

"How do you know that for sure?" Marcia asked lightly, noticing the empty flatness was on the left side of the seam.

"Well, that's what I meant before when I was telling you about section fifty-three C of the building code. Nobody's ever tried this before. They can't put these people in public housing. Look what happened at Columbia Point."

"Oh," said Marcia. She wondered if he actually placed it

on the right side or if it accidentally fell there or if it ever got caught in between. "Do you do other stuff than this housing or are you concentrating just on this?" she asked.

"I don't have time. Why should I? I'm going into this anyway." Jerry sat back. Marcia was afraid she had lost him.

"The thing I don't understand though," she said desperately, "is section fifty-three C."

Jerry crossed his legs. "Well, it's difficult to explain," he said. "Are you sure you want me to go into it?"

"Yes, I'd love to know. I mean it's so important and it's the key to the whole thing," she said. It was still on the right side of the seam. Marcia wondered if he ever sat on it. She wondered what Jerry would do, what Carla and John and the other bespectacled law student would do if she ran over and grabbed it, just for a second. Jerry's words circled by. She looked him straight in the eye for a moment. It would be the absolute end of her. The police would be called. She would be placed in an insane asylum for the rest of her life. Marcia shivered because she was sure she had come within a sliver of doing just that. Although she had once seen a naked baby boy, and she knew it was in three parts, she could see only two clearly outlined. Was Jerry missing one? No, he'd have a high voice if he were, that much she knew. Carol told her they changed sizes; she didn't know when, however, and Marcia started to worry that it might change size right there in front of her. How could she pretend not to notice? Jerry would know she had been staring. She couldn't understand a bit of what he was saying. He smiled at her. His teeth were even and white. She heard herself telling Carol, *"God, when he smiled, I mean it made me want to jump right out of my seat and I felt this strange . . ."*

Marcia accepted another glass of sherry. Her boots dripped enormous puddles in front of her chair but she didn't dare take them off for fear her feet would be sooty and hideous underneath.

Jerry asked her if she was planning to go to law school. No, she hadn't made up her mind. She would make a good lawyer, he observed, because she was a good listener. But it would be better if she decided to do something else because law school was awful, bar exams were worse. Still, all the jobs were going to women and blacks these days, so it would be simple. His words tripped easily in and out of Marcia's mind. She was almost sure, at times, that he was making no sense at all, except he was a law student and she was only Marcia so he must be making sense, but she didn't really mind not understanding him. She was memorizing his arms, the three blue veins on the top of his hands, the soft red hairs stopping just at the knuckles. She wondered if he burned or tanned in the sun.

She imagined him, almost naked, on a white hot beach in front of a brilliant sea. She sat in a small half-moon of shadow under a striped umbrella and waited for him to run across the sand and find her. The heat waves from the sand dissolved him into a watery black blur against the sky, and the minutes that it took him to reach her slowed to a breathless drugged expanse that she could speed up or leave be at will. When at last she brought him into clear view—dark brown and covered with speckles of salt, smiling and just reaching down for her— she stopped her thinking abruptly, telling herself furiously how wrong it was to daydream this way.

She did little else that night, however, until she got out of bed, disgusted with herself, and let the freezing air from an open window distract her and strip the heat from her face.

"Did you have a nice time?"

"Yeah, great time. I'm sleepy though," said Marcia, yawning. "If *she* wasn't so uptight about my homework, I wouldn't have had to get up so early. There was a later train at—"

"Buy anything for yourself?" her father asked.

"No, I still have about forty dollars left."

Marcia's father grunted as he struggled with the steering wheel. "You're a good kid, honey," he said. "Not a spendthrift. We've got to get a new car with a standard shift. This thing doesn't do well in the snow. I can't get any traction." He grunted again as the wheels spun without effect in the gravel and ice. Then he dropped his hands in disgust and stared out the window at the flat, snowy air. "Sharon came home," he said shyly.

"She did? When?"

"Yesterday. She's not home at the moment. How are Carla and John?"

"They're fine," said Marcia. "Where did Sharon go?"

"She's in New York at the moment."

"New *York!*"

"She . . . we had a disagreement, that is your mother . . . Mother and I. Sharon said she didn't want to cause a fight."

"But why?"

"Now calm down. I said it would be up to Sharon, whatever she wanted to do, and she went. She went down on a plane yesterday. I paid for it. It was her decision." He turned the key in the ignition. The engine made a sick whirring noise. "Flooded," he said sadly.

"Daddy, why did you have a fight? What's wrong with Sharon? Why did she come home again?"

"We may have to get out and push. Do you have boots on? Yes, you do."

"Daddy, *tell* me!"

"Well, it seems Mother thought it would be better all around for you and Chrissy if Sharon stayed in Florida."

"But why? Why did she say that?"

"Now listen. I didn't agree with her."

A heavy vapor formed on the windows. Marcia wiped at it with her pocketbook. "Daddy, will you please tell me what happened. Sharon knows better than to come back."

"Well, you know Mother. It seems Sharon is . . . was going to have a baby. She's only two months gone."

"She's pregnant! But Buddy's been away almost a year!"

"I know. I think Sharon knows she did wrong. I talked to her. She said she'd never do it again. She promised."

"She's pregnant and Mother threw her out? What is she going to do?"

"Well, we settled that. I got Mother to agree that we should pay for . . . pay to have things settled."

"Pay for an abortion, you mean."

"Well, yes. She's at the best clinic in New York City right now so you mustn't worry about her."

"But why couldn't she keep it? Why, Daddy?"

"She said her husband . . . she said Buddy . . . well, she said he'd kill her if he found out, and of course that's ridiculous and I told her so and she agreed, finally, that he was not a violent person. She was just using a figure of speech. But apparently things hadn't been all that good between them before he left for Vietnam. You know young people have to expect some troubles, and she said he'd probably divorce her if he found out. She didn't want to take a chance on being a divorcée with a baby. So we felt this was the best thing to do under the circumstances."

"Daddy, you can't even say the word abortion, can you?"

"I didn't want to hurt you. I didn't know if you knew about things like that."

Marcia smirked despite the panic rising in her stomach. She looked over at her father. He was breathing heavily. She wanted to shake him, but he was such a bland little man in such a bland gray car coat that she simply asked, "Why did Mother throw her out? How come—"

"She said what Sharon did is immoral, and, of course, she's right there. She said she doesn't want that kind of thing around Chrissy or you, that she never bargained for it. Believe me I had a hard time talking her into the clinic. She doesn't believe in them either. She said Sharon should have the baby and stay in Florida. We compromised. She agreed that Sharon should have . . . should go to New York and she agreed never to tell Buddy about it. She's also letting her stay home tonight. As soon as I drop you off I'm going down to pick her up."

"Big of her."

Her father slammed the car door. Marcia watched him kicking the spongy snow outside. "Looking for a rock flat enough for us to get some traction," he said with an apologetic grin. He found two and shoved them under the back wheels of the car. This time the motor turned over reluctantly and the wheels caught on the rocks. They drove out of the parking lot in someone else's tracks.

"That's real big of her," Marcia said again.

"Don't be so emotional, honey. I know how you feel but you have to look at the other side of the picture and understand her too."

"Her!"

"I think she's done wonders with you, you know. Look at your schoolwork."

"You had a bad fight, didn't you?" said Marcia slowly.

"Of course not."

"She said some things about Mamma again, I bet. I know what she thinks. She thinks I'm going to be just like Sharon if she dooesn't keep her clutches in me."

"She didn't say that, honey. You're making things up."

"She threatened to leave you if Sharon got to stay home."

"No."

"Daddy, you won't even say the word *abortion*. What do you think is happening? You think Sharon's getting . . . she's getting a hangnail taken off or something?"

"It's the only answer. Let's not talk about it."

"What's this about not wanting my own sister around me, or around precious Chrissy?"

Her father's voice was unsteady. He clutched the steering wheel with both hands at the top as if he were driving at a hideous speed on a raceway, but the needle didn't register above twenty-five. "I was thinking about getting a new Dodge," he said.

"A new *Dodge?*"

"You'll be getting your learner's permit soon. How would you like to have this car for your very own?"

"I don't want a car. I want to know what happened."

"I told you what happened. Now let's let bygones be bygones."

"Daddy, how could you marry her?" Marcia asked almost inaudibly. She didn't even mean for him to answer that.

"She's a fine woman. I love her."

"I hate her!"

He turned to look at her, wide-eyed and serious. "Don't say the word *hate*. Never use the word *hate*," he cautioned, waggling a gloved finger in Marcia's direction.

"I'm going down there to live with Sharon. I'm going down to take care of my sister."

"No," he said. "You're not."

"Says who?"

"Don't sass me, honey. There are things in life you don't understand yet. Mother's doing a terrific job with you. Your schoolwork is up a hundred percent. You may even be able to go to college. You may not believe this at first, and it might be a little hard to take, but in some ways she's probably a better mother than Mamma was. I don't mean better. It's just that Mamma couldn't help some things. But I don't think you would have gone to college if she'd lived and I'm beginning to think that might not be such a bad idea. You can meet nice boys. Someone with a future. That's better than you'll do around here, getting a job with only a high school diploma."

"What do you mean, 'Mamma couldn't help some things'?"

"Nothing. Nothing at all."

"Daddy, you must have meant *something* by it."

He slowed the car down even more. "Well," he began, "Mamma was a wonderful person. A wonderful, wonderful person. You know she was very different from Sparky—from Mother—I mean. She was different to you and different to me . . . she . . . well, she loved you and Sharon as much . . . as much as anyone could love anyone else, but she never . . . she never wanted anything much for you, either of you. I can see things now that I didn't see before. Mother cares about things, and maybe I was remiss. Maybe I should have done different, especially with . . . with your sister. If Mother had had Sharon from your age, maybe Sharon wouldn't be where she is now. Mother is a wonderful person too, and she . . . she's gotten me doing things. That was her idea to go to Europe for our honeymoon. I probably never would have gone in my whole life. She reads newspapers. She even has me going to town meetings now. You know I never did anything like that when Mamma was alive."

"Town meetings!" said Marcia, glowering at the dashboard.

"Honey, it's not just town meetings. It's . . . well, she's *alive!* She has lots of pep. Mamma . . . Mamma was very different. She . . . well, we got married when we were both only eighteen, right out of high school. Then when I got back from the navy and your sister was born, she changed. She slowed down a lot. Of course she was sick. I'm not saying . . ."

"You're saying she fizzled out. Is that it?"

"Oh, honey, I loved Mamma. You know that. But I'm happy now too. Don't you want your daddy to be happy?"

"Of *course* I do, Daddy. I'm sorry. It's just that—"

"Now run in and give Mother a hug. She's upset too," he said, pulling carefully into the driveway.

"Daddy, you've got to be kidding! You know what she says about that. She never can . . . what does she say? . . . show any kind of affection, physically, for any kids but her own? You've *heard* her say that. Like it was a rule or something."

Her father looked around wildly. He, of all people, never required her to say the right thing, to say anything at all, for that matter. Marcia knew she had hurt him somehow. "Honey, I love you," he said shakily. "People are weak, sometimes, I guess. Sometimes they don't do what you want them to, and this is hard on all of us, so please try not to make her any angrier."

"Okay, okay."

As he turned off the ignition, he added, "The money you have left . . . from what I gave you. You can keep that, you know. Spend it any way you like."

Sharon's bed had reappeared in the room. Mother bent over it, making her crisp hospital corners.

"We've moved this back up for the night," she said. "You don't mind sleeping with your sister? I thought she shouldn't be down on the couch alone."

Marcia said nothing. She dropped her suitcase upside down on a chair and opened a bureau drawer aimlessly.

"Marcia, I know you must be angry with me about Sharon. Your father has probably told you."

"Where is she now? Is she having it done?"

"Yes. Your father's calling for her this afternoon. She could have stayed there one more night and taken the plane, but I thought it would be nicer—"

"I'm going with him."

"Have you finished your homework?"

"Homework?"

"Have you finished your homework? It's five hours down and five hours back. You won't be home till eight o'clock."

Marcia seized a freshly ironed blouse from the drawer. She dropped it on the floor in a heap and lay face down on her bed. She could feel Mother's restraint at this tingling in the air behind her.

"Marcia, if she were my daughter, I would do the same thing."

"She's not and neither am I."

"No, Sharon's not. But you hurt me when you say that. I . . . consider you my own daughter."

"Yeah."

"Marcia, when Sharon is not here, things go very smoothly. Somehow there are nothing but arguments when she's around. Do you like that? Do you want to live that way?"

"I don't care."

"Marcia, I want the best for you, just as I do for Chrissy. Your father and I agreed about this. It's the best thing for all of us."

Mother yanked the bedspread over Sharon's bed. She waited for Marcia to answer. "Do you know what Sharon has done?" she asked after an interval. "Do you understand about this kind of thing? I've never had a talk with you about . . . this." There was no movement in Marcia's shoulders. "Well it happens. Even in this day and age with pills. I hope you know enough never to do it." She picked up the blouse and refolded it.

"Your mother probably never talked to Sharon about this, but I'm talking to you. Do you hear me?" She slammed the drawer shut. "Do you hear me, Marcia?" Marcia knew Mother would not dare joggle her arm. She would only yell for a while and then she would be finished—over and away down the word drain. "She's lucky, Sharon is. She's lucky her husband isn't going to know. She's lucky she has people to take care of her. She's lucky she didn't catch anything. Do you know you can catch diseases doing that? There are two kinds, syphilis and gonorrhea. Syphilis causes insanity in eighty percent of the cases. Incurable insanity."

Marcia opened her eyes. The tufts of the bedspread were out of focus. She stared at the top of her hand.

"Your sister's destroying a human life. Do you understand that? It was your father's idea, not mine . . . Why don't you say something?"

"There's nothing to say," Marcia whispered.

"What was that? I didn't hear you."

"Nothing."

"Marcia, you're hurting me terribly. I would do the same thing with my own daughter, if Sharon were mine. I don't want you to grow up with that around you . . . things like that. She told your father that husband of hers would kill her if he found out. Neither of us believed that, but I don't want . . . I don't want people like that around! Can't you see? She'll be all right. She'll go back to Florida and get a job. Please try to accept that."

"Okay."

"Not just 'okay!' "

"I have a stomachache now." Marcia turned away from the wall. Her face was white, but she had not cried.

. . .

"What do you think, Princess? You think it's going to snow all day?"

"I don't know, Daddy."

"We could have let her stay over another night in the clinic, you know. But I told her we'd pick her up. I hope she'll be comfortable in the back."

Marcia's eyes followed the two windshield wipers as they slushed the wet snow back and forth across the glass. Each flake in the headlight beams looked as if it had been hurled individually at them with tremendous force. She wished her father would be his usual silent self so she could look at the snow.

"Mother put a lot of pillows and blankets back there," he remarked. Marcia pretended to be asleep.

"Got you out of the house without your homework," he said, chuckling. "The teachers won't be too mad tomorrow, will they? You can always say your sister was . . . sick." He lit his pipe.

"It's okay, Daddy. One day won't hurt."

"Sure enough it won't hurt. You're doing so good now I'm proud of you. Mamma would have been proud too. All those college kids in your classes. You're doing better than Chrissy, almost."

Marcia laughed a short laugh to please him and looked out her side window. She could hear the pride in his voice and she knew he meant what he said, but she wondered why he had waited until today to mention it. She hated herself for hearing his grammatical errors. She supposed she'd been noticing them for some time now without wanting to admit it. He never bothered with anything fancy, he said often enough, not that her father wasn't smart. He worked for a large company called General Precision, which he called "the firm." He had something to do with computers or numbers, she didn't really know what. They had shipped him from their Fall River branch to their Beverley branch at his request when he had married Mother. He had been so thrilled that day, she remembered, not to have to change his job. He had spent twenty years in a gray metal office filled with machines. Whether he fixed them or ran them she did not know. Marcia and Sharon had visited there once, when they were little. The offices had reminded her of an ancient school building, with their yellow ceiling lights and worn wooden floors. Marcia had played with a doll in his office, carefully dressing and undressing it, as her father, flushed with some unusual afternoon energy, introduced Sharon to the people working around him. Marcia had not looked at anything. There had been nothing to look at. Sharon was twelve at the time. She was considered the smart one. She knew how to please grown-ups with her quick answers. Marcia was called the quiet one. Sharon had pigtails with plaid bows at the ends. Sharon.

She's like a blown-out egg, Marcia thought, with the shell still intact and just a tiny hole where everything ran through. They helped Sharon out of the waiting room.

"I'm really fine," she protested. "They gave me some pills and everything." Her father had held the sleeve of Sharon's coat as if it were a piece of soft glass that might explode or do something horrible at any moment.

Sharon sniffed. "It was nothing at all," she said. "I hardly felt a thing." She had tried to laugh.

"Can you make it home all right, honey, do you think? It's going to be a long drive but I'll go slow—avoid the potholes."

"Yeah, I'm fine. I just took a pill. I'll probably sleep. What did *she* say?"

"Nothing," said her father. "Now watch these steps. She

was real nice and fixed up your bed and everything. Everybody feels terrible."

"Hunhh!" said Sharon. "I bet she does."

"We won't talk about it. You can stay home till you're better."

"I'm not going back there. I can stay here in New York in a hotel."

"Hotel!" Her father glanced around desperately at the few passing people in the street. "You're coming home where we can take care of you," he said.

"Maybe we could all stay in a hotel," Marcia suggested, but her father had opened the car door and gently pushed Sharon down on the back seat. "No arguments now, no arguments," he had said laughingly again and again, until he closed the back door and jumped into the driver's seat as if it was a getaway car.

Marcia was itching to ask her sister how it felt. Was she awake while they did it? Was it alive? Did she see it? Did she close her eyes? Sharon asked if there was a country-western radio station in the area. Marcia fiddled with the dial and found a sawing, whining sound that approximated country-western.

"That's all they listen to down in Florida," Sharon said huskily. "You sort of get used to it."

"Well, I hope you can find a good job down there," said her father.

"Oh, I'm sure I will. I can type. I can work a switchboard."

"That's right. Those things come in handy." He turned to Marcia. "Maybe you could take typing extra now that you're not in the General Course anymore," he said. "Typing is always the key to a good job."

Marcia said nothing. The snow had become a solid, black rain that swept the car clean and glistening. He was not himself. Marcia did not like to see her father troubled and nervous. Most of the time he said so little, but when he was disturbed, he always said too much. It had been like that during the time her mother was sick. The trips to the hospital had worn him ragged. Sharon had had to remind him to shave. "In emergencies a girl can always make money with typing and switchboard," he continued. "College degrees are a dime a dozen. You never know when there's going to be another depression. Everybody's heard about '29—all those people with college educations were jumping out of windows." His voice trailed off as a truck sailed past them at eighty miles an hour. "Is she asleep?" he asked in a different voice.

Marcia glanced into the back seat. She could see Sharon's pallor, even in the flashing yellow of passing headlights. One small manicured hand rested lightly on the pink blanket covering her stomach. Her lips were slightly open. It can't be Sharon, Marcia thought. Usually Sharon slept in a petulant bundle, her face to the wall. Now she looked like a newspaper picture of a rape victim. "I think she's dropped off," said Marcia. "Shall I turn the radio off."

"Turn it off. I can't listen to that stuff."

"Do you think she'll wake up? I mean does that pill make you unconscious?"

"I don't think so. She needs sleep."

Her father seemed to have gained back some stability now that he didn't have to contend with Sharon directly. He pulled on his pipe dreamily and drove with one hand. "I hope this is the last time this ever happens to her," he said, indicating Sharon with the stem of his pipe. "I hope it never happens to you."

"It won't, Daddy."

"You know about . . . Mother, has she told you about . . . what you ought to know?"

"Yes, I know about it, Daddy."

"Your, uh, time of the month . . . all that . . . you know about all that?"

"Four years ago, Daddy, *please*."

"I guess Mamma was alive."

Marcia sighed. "No," she said patiently. "She had already died. Or maybe she was in the hospital. I forget."

"You were all alone when . . . that happened to you?"

"Shar was there. I had her."

"Did Sharon . . . has Mother told you everything you need to know?"

"Can we *drop* the subject, Daddy?"

Her father drove in hopeless silence for many minutes. Then he said, "I guess you'd like it better if Sharon stayed. I mean if she lived with us till Buddy gets home."

Marcia looked the other way. "What's the use of talking about it?" she said.

"Mother does try to help, you know. In her own way she's very fond of you."

"She gets on me. Why don't you tell her not to get on me? My clothes are too tight . . . my marks . . . my friends. Nothing's right. Whatever Chrissy does is right and until I'm like Chrissy she'll never be happy—and I'll never be like Chrissy."

"That isn't altogether true. She wishes Chrissy dressed neat like you and things. She doesn't like Chrissy being such a tomboy at fifteen. She worries about Chrissy too."

"She'd worry about Jesus Christ himself."

"Don't swear, honey."

"What are you going to do?" Marcia asked, although she didn't want to keep talking at all. "Get Mother to let Sharon stay?"

"Nothing. I don't know."

"You say Sharon's leaving is *her* decision. Mother says it's *your* decision. Nothing's anybody's fault. Nothing seems to rest where it belongs. People say things and the next thing you know they're blaming someone else for saying it."

"No one's blaming anybody, honey. We're not trying to lay blame."

"Oh, forget it," said Marcia wearily.

"This is a terrible thing that Sharon has done. I don't believe in . . . in what she had to do."

"Then how come you went along with it?"

"It seemed to be the easiest thing, that's all. But it leads to more and more immorality. Just like dope. Everything leads to more, these days. Everything's changed. I don't know. It's over. Let's forget it." He drove for a little while and then pulled over to the side of the road and got out. Sharon woke up. "What's he doing?" she asked. "Where are we?"

"I don't know," said Marcia. "I think he's getting sick or something." She felt Sharon's hand rest on her shoulder and heard her say, "You take care of Daddy, now." Then she lay back on the pillow and went to sleep.

Chrissy tiptoed into the doorway. "How is she?" she whispered.

"Okay, I guess. She's gone to sleep again. It's very late and she's had a long day," Marcia said. "She won't eat." Marcia sat on the side of her sister's bed, holding a tray of untouched dinner. A balanced meal, she thought, looking at the soup and salad. Mother had made some tapioca. What a thing! Marcia said to herself. Mother had even gone to the store and bought a jar of maraschino cherries so that there would be one cherry on top of the pudding. To Marcia's knowledge, there had never been a jar of maraschino cherries in the house before.

"Is she . . . is she bleeding?" Chrissy asked hoarsely.

Marcia got up with the tray. She felt much older than

Chrissy. She didn't want to answer questions about Sharon's privacy—about her secret parts bleeding into the night.

"C'mere!" Chrissy beckoned Marcia into her room.

Marcia held the tray awkwardly against her hip. "What?" she asked.

"Hey, Marsh, I heard what Mom said to you this morning. I mean, I didn't listen in or anything but I couldn't help hearing. I just wanted to tell you I was on your side. I think Mom was awful and I told her so."

"Thanks," said Marcia dryly. She turned to take the tray downstairs.

"No, stay," said Chrissy.

"What?"

"Well, what was it like? Did she tell you?

"Yes."

"Well?"

"It wasn't too bad."

"C'mon, Marsh. You can tell me. I'm your sister."

Chrissy had never said that before. Marcia almost laughed. "Well, then. Sharon's your sister too," she said. "Go ask her."

"I can't. I mean she's asleep and everything. Listen . . ." Chrissy hesitated and then sat on the bed with her hands clasped righteously in her lap. "Mom never tells me anything," she said. "Except about diseases and tubes and eggs and stuff. You probably think I'm awfully dumb but I don't know anything really and I thought you could tell me a little more. I mean the only person I can talk to is Jenny and she doesn't know any more than I do."

Marcia shifted the tray to the other hip. She laughed inside— a long satisfying laugh at Chrissy and Jenny and their horses, their tennis tournaments, and their A grades. Magic Jennifer, so thin, with her hair parted in the middle like a Madonna, her straight perfect teeth, and those long sensitive fingers. She,

Marcia, had some power in this area. It was very important to Chrissy, she could see that in her face.

"It hurt her, mostly afterward, she says," Marcia said. "Otherwise, they just put her in a little white room, everybody has their own private room and waits, and then they wheeled her on this bed to the operating room and they gave her a shot and they took this thing and they pulled it on out. She doesn't remember well. They gave her something to make her go to sleep and then she came home."

"But what do they do with it? Is it alive?"

"I don't know."

"Do they let you see it?"

"I wouldn't think so."

"Gee."

"I don't know any more, Chris."

"Well, thanks."

"Any time."

Marcia took the tray down to the kitchen.

"She didn't eat," Mother said anxiously.

"She wasn't hungry."

"I was hoping she might like the tapioca. I thought something light and cool . . . How is she?"

"She's asleep." Marcia began to take the things off the tray. She put them one by one into the refrigerator. She felt like a nurse. Everyone was so worried about Sharon suddenly, but no one went near her but Marcia.

"Is she all right?" Mother asked.

"I guess so."

"Is she . . . is she still bleeding?"

"I don't know. What do you want me to do? Wake her up and ask her?"

"Marcia, I'm sorry I was a little hard on you this morning. I can get like that—I—"

"That's all right. I'm going to do my homework now. Then I'll go to bed."

"Good . . . good. Let me know if there's anything . . . if she . . . if Sharon needs anything."

Marcia tried to concentrate on her schoolwork. She managed to get through her geometry problems without too much trouble. They were fast and clean and she could leave off and look at her sister now and then. But she found herself reading the same sentence over and over again in her history book without making any sense of it. It annoyed her that someone who had previously owned her textbook had underlined certain passages in red. Marcia didn't know whether they were important to this year's teacher or not. They distracted her. She wondered if she could run off to Florida the next day, taking Sharon down, somehow taking care of her. If only these last two years of high school were not sitting in front of her like a wall that took just so long to climb. Sharon lay on her back, and Marcia was once again struck with her sister's unusual position. She always lay on her side. She leafed backward through the grubby pages of her book to the beginning of the chapter she was supposed to read for a test. There was a discussion of economic forces before the Civil War, something too about the Dred Scott decision. She looked at a picture of a slave market and then read down the list of names scrawled on the inside of the endpaper. She tried to imagine the people who had owned this book in years past. They were all out in the real world now, doing something. This book had been through the ten-month school year with all of them. It had come home at night to how many different houses? And stayed behind in a closet only to start the same sophomore year again with somebody else. She looked at the chapter titles "A House Divided," "The Nation Binds Its Wounds." This book, Marcia decided, had bored many people.

She packed her suitcase silently, not even wanting to wake her sister. She took out her bathing suit with a small shock of guilt, but Florida did have beautiful blue-green water to swim in, and why not? After all. She could get a job or go to high school down there, see to it her sister wasn't lonely, that she stayed out of trouble . . . she could take her sister to the beach.

Her head filled with lovely airy plans for Florida and it took her over an hour to fall asleep, but when she awoke in the morning, Sharon had already gone.

Sixteen

· 1 ·

"Raymond Siroken's going to ask you to a party."

"You're kidding."

"No, I'm not kidding. He likes you."

"He's going to be a senior."

"So?"

Marcia chewed her lip thoughtfully. "Well, it's June anyway, so I guess it'll be a onetime thing and he'll be over it by the time school starts again," she said.

Carol sighed dramatically. "I don't know what it is with you," she said. "Here the cutest guy in the whole school likes you and you don't want to give him the time of day."

"It's not that," said Marcia. "It's just that . . . well, he's sort of going with Betty Thompson, isn't he? And besides, that whole crowd—I couldn't ever get in with that crowd."

"You wait," said Carol, ambling into her driveway. "I wish I were going. It should be a neat party. It's at Jimmy Goslau's house and they have a pool and everything."

"He hasn't even asked me," said Marcia, shaking her head and laughing.

"Well, a word to the wise," said Carol. "By the way, have you made up your mind about a summer job yet?"

"I don't know. I'm supposed to go to this interview Mother wants me to go to I told you about."

"Yeah, but did I tell you I got a letter from Speedy Set? I thought all the kids did. I'm going down there Monday. Why don't you come?"

"I got the letter, but Mother'd have a cow. Besides, you can't make any money that way, can you?"

"You sure can. You get a dollar a set and tips from the ladies and you get to work when you want. That's about ten, eleven dollars a day, sixty dollars a week, and I don't know— if you work a hundred hours or something, you get to be a Junior Beautician, for whatever that's worth."

"I'll think about it."

"Well, let me know."

Free Carol. Marcia envied her. Carol's mother was so easy-going, never made a big thing out of Carol's friends, her grades, the kind of summer job she wanted. "Carol's parents don't seem to care *what* she does!" Mother had said one time in reference to something trivial . . . the tightness of Carol's pants was it? Or how many Cokes she drank? The implication was that this would someday result in disastrous consequences for Carol. Marcia remembered now. According to Mother, if you left your teeth in a glass of Coke overnight they would be gone, dissolved by morning. So Carol's Coke drinking would probably wind her up in the poorhouse from dentist's bills or at least as an old maid from having false teeth at the age of twenty. Still, Mother didn't object to Carol as much as she had to Lynn. She seemed to think Carol was a step along the way to yet "nicer" friends. Jennies? No, Marcia thought. I could never be friends with anyone like Jenny. She was not looking forward to her interview with Mrs. Whaley.

Mother had suggested that since Marcia could not teach riding like Chrissy, she become a mother's helper, and Mrs. Whaley was just the person. Marcia had seen Mrs. Whaley around town in previous summers. The Whaleys came up from the city and rented the same house every year from people who went off mountain climbing. Mrs. Whaley's husband was a doctor, and although they were summer people, Mother approved of them heartily. Good influences, Marcia thought, a house filled with books and important things to read. Did Mother expect these piles of written words to fly into Marcia's head of their own accord? Mrs. Whaley was the mother of two irritating, doughy little girls, and Marcia did not like the idea of taking care of them.

She thought again about Raymond. That would not sit too well at home either. There was no way in which she could prevent Mother from hearing stories about him. Mother would not like his casual, slouching manner, his slightly slanted green eyes. She wouldn't think he was good looking, although all the girls thought he looked just like Robert Redford. Why am I worrying about this? Marcia asked herself. He hasn't even asked me, and he probably won't . . . but if I went out with Raymond Siroken . . . if I. . . . She began to picture herself among his crowd, the boys no longer staring deliberately past her as they stood outside the school smoking, but giving her a little nod of recognition because she was Raymie's girl. She would automatically be able to walk to classes with Sue Sturgiss and Penny Loomis, varsity cheerleaders, all laughing under their breath in a secret language, swinging their pocketbooks—and their bottoms—ever so tantalizingly to boys and girls alike. Marcia thought suddenly about Carla and what Carla would think of this. It was the other side of the world, she knew that much.

Mrs. Whaley was a stubby, frank little woman who picked bits of tobacco off her tongue as she talked. She offered Marcia thirty dollars a week.

"My husband will be home all summer," she said, "and we'll be going to the beach and doing a lot of sailing, but it's too much for the girls. I want you to keep them outside. Keep them away from the television. They're indoors practically all year in Boston. And you know, there'll be just a little housework now and then if I need you in a pinch."

Marcia looked away from Mrs. Whaley into the interior of this very expensive house. Whoever the mountain climbers might be, they were probably just like the Whaleys since the house seemed to fit Mrs. Whaley exactly. One of the children was screaming in a back room.

"Excuse me a moment. That's Lisa. She's not always like this."

"Oh, sure. It's all right."

"Sit down," said Mrs. Whaley. "I'll be right back."

Marcia sank deeply into a square white sofa. She heard Mrs. Whaley murmuring something somewhere in the house. A statue next to Marcia resembled a giant melting ice mountain. Marcia touched it, but of course it was glass, not ice. Lisa whined and sobbed, but Mrs. Whaley did not yell at her. She spoke in a smooth undervoice like a radio announcer. Marcia felt herself tighten in the comfortable sofa. This was yet another kind of living—something she had not seen close up before. There were no lamps on the tables, only partly hidden light cylinders stuck at angles in the ceiling and one huge lamp with five chrome tendrils set in a Mexican flowerpot near the fireplace. The room was so peaceful. Marcia supposed it hid all sounds, even arguments, in its heavy brown carpets. She wondered what people did in this room. Her stomach began to tighten, so she left.

"Well, how did it go?" Mother asked cheerfully.

"Uh . . . I don't know. She says she's going to call me back. She might have a couple of other girls to interview."

"Who? Anybody you know from school?"

"How should I know?"

"Marcia!"

"I'm sorry. I just don't know. She says she'll call back."

"Well, did you give a good impression? Do you think you made a favorable impression?"

Marcia tried to edge her way out of the kitchen, but Mother was polishing the telephone in the doorway. She considered going out the way she had come in. "I don't know," she said, remembering that she had been asked a question.

"Did she ask you for references? Did you give her our phone number so that she can talk to me if she wants?"

"No. I mean yes. I'm going down for another interview with Carol, Monday."

Mother placed the receiver back in its gleaming cradle. "For what job?"

"Well, there's a place in town called Speedy Set where you can make sixty dollars a week."

"Doing what, may I ask?"

"Well, learning how to set hair and give manicures and everything and after a hundred hours you get to be a junior beautician."

"A junior beautician."

"Yes. Well, Carol says so anyway."

"And you want to be a beautician. First a stewardess and now a beautician."

"Mother, it's only a summer job. I'd be making twice, three times as much as Chrissy."

"No."

"What do you mean *no?*" Marcia felt her throat contract. She tried to coax her stomach into submission.

"You're not going to be in a beauty parlor all summer long with all those girls and chemicals. No means no. You can forget about it right now."

The last thing Marcia said before leaving the house was "I'm asking Daddy!" but she knew it would do no good. She paced along the retaining wall by the bay for almost an hour before she realized where she was. She looked up and saw a black Cadillac whiz by and thought in a panic that it might be Mrs. Whaley. What would she think? Would she call Mother? Would Mother call her? Marcia started walking very quickly toward the center of town. She would go to Speedy Set and apply for the job right away. Maybe they would say yes today. Carol said it was easy. She straightened her clothes and combed her hair as best she could with her fingers. She had walked out of the house without a pocketbook. Still, maybe they wouldn't notice.

The street ran along an old part of town where the postcard pictures were taken. It was supposed to be beautiful, but Marcia was annoyed at the constantly wheeling gulls and the seedy old buildings that stank of fish. A statue of a sou'westered fisherman leaned blindly into an invisible storm, and Marcia squinted up at his face for the hundredth time, wondering again why people never bothered to put eyeballs in statues.

Speedy Set was closed on Saturdays. Marcia knew that when she saw the darkened window three blocks away, but she walked the three blocks anyway and gazed in between the blue plastic screens and read the sign: *Beauty School 1 Fl. up. Accred. Mass. Inst. Beau. Sci.* Institute of Beauty Science sounded respectable enough, but it would not impress Mother. Marcia wandered slowly up the street, past Siroken's Garage.

Raymond looked up from an open truck hood. "Hi," he said.

"Hi," said Marcia. He did look like Robert Redford, she told herself.

"What are you doing in this part of town?"

"Oh, I don't know. I was going to apply for a job, but they're closed." Marcia wanted to kick herself for sounding so stupid. "I mean I went to see if they were open," she added.

"Yeah, where?" Raymond stood up and assumed his full slouch, the one all the popular boys used. He wiped his oil-embedded fingers easily, one at a time, on a greasy rag. He was a dark blond. He must have to shave a lot, Marcia thought, noticing the stubble on his face. She caught herself watching him breathe, fascinated.

"Oh, just a beauty shop," she said. "Carol Kubiak and I were thinking of working there. It's called Speedy Set. It's supposed to pay pretty well." Marcia sensed that the subject of making money would be a safe one with Raymond.

Raymond sounded bored, however. "Penny tried that last year, she told me," he said. "Maybe it was last year. Anyway, she said it was a ripoff . . . only lasted a week. She said the people who go into that place only do it to save a few bucks and they don't tip a dime."

"Oh," said Marcia hopelessly.

"Yeah, but I know where there's a good job. I mean if you're looking for a good job."

"Where?"

"Taylor's. They need a waitress."

"But I don't have any experience."

"They don't need that, it says in the door. There's a sign up. Whyn't you ask anyway? It'd pay better than any old beauty shop."

"Well, thanks. I'll go over and see."

Raymond smiled a half-crooked smile and walked backward toward his truck engine. "See you Friday," he said, throwing a rag expertly into a can twenty feet away.

"Friday?"

"Six. I'll pick you up. There's a party at Jimmy's."

"But I mean—"

"So you don't want to come with me?"

"What? No. I mean it was just that you didn't ask and everything and—"

"So I have to ask?"

"I just . . . I just . . . okay, I'll see you," said Marcia. She was a little frightened, but she remembered to say thank you over her shoulder as she walked back into town, which was more, it occurred to her, than she had done for Mrs. Whaley.

She waited in a cluttered, windowless little office in the back of Taylor's diner trying to keep her mind on the interview ahead of her and not on Raymond, his silver Rough Rider's belt buckle, the two tiny medals which dangled in the hair of his already sunburned chest. She wondered if she could get a tan in time for Friday night's party. The June sun in Massachusetts was not strong. Someone called Gloria was in the middle of an interminable telephone conversation outside the door, but no one came in to interview her. Gloria had told her to wait in a chair. Marcia sat with her knees together, looking hopefully out the doorway every few seconds and occasionally at Gloria, who took no notice of her whatever. She waved off the flies that settled around her, hoping she would not be seen in case someone thought she was being critical. Did Raymond and his crowd think this was an all right place to work, or had he suggested it just trying to be nice? He didn't seem like the kind of person who would just up and be nice, however.

Mr. Taylor strode in suddenly, introducing himself and stressing the mister very hard. He had a pencil behind each ear and said he didn't have much time. Marcia tried not to look at his greasy apron.

"Forty-five a week with tips. You should do all right. Ever waited before?" he asked.

Marcia didn't know whether to stand and offer him the chair. She decided not to. "No, this is my first job actually," she said.

"What are you? High school? I thought you were older."

"Yes, I'm a junior. Or at least I will be in September."

Mr. Taylor grunted. "Gloria get off that damn horn, will you!" he snapped. "Well, you gotta be here on time. No lateness. You understand?"

"Yes, Mr. Taylor. I'll be on time. I'm never late."

"Gotta boyfriend?"

"No. Why, do you think—"

"No fooling around giving extra Cokes, freebies. No messing around talking to your friends who come in here. Understand?"

"Yes, sir."

"Or you're out on your ear."

"Yes, sir."

"I had a high school kid here before. Tried to give all her friends free stuff. Thought I wouldn't notice. Loused up my cooking. Wasted thirty dollars worth of Fry-Max on me."

Marcia waited him out.

"I wouldn't hire you except I got a girl just left and this is my busy season. Somebody comes along with more experience, you go. Understand?"

"Yes, I understand."

"Still want the job?"

"Yes, I do."

"Go see Gloria about your hours. And I don't want no sneakers or bare legs in here. Stockings and shoes. There's uniforms out in the kitchen. She'll show you." Mr. Taylor vanished as swiftly as he had appeared.

Marcia waited as Gloria chattered away with the diner's one customer. Gloria spoke and gestured slowly but she snapped her chewing gum furiously. Suddenly she turned to Marcia, who had been too afraid to interrupt.

"See that!" Gloria shouted triumphantly, pointing to the transom over the front door.

"Yes?" said Marcia, uncertain what she was supposed to look at.

"Sam's idea of air conditioning! Can you beat that?"

"Oh, yes," said Marcia blankly.

Gloria chuckled at the man in front of her drinking coffee. He was trying to make a nickel stand on end. "I ask you," she said. Then she muttered some more and made a show of cleaning the counter top. "Well, I guess I have to show you around," she said to no one in particular.

"Well, Mr. Taylor said if you're not busy . . ."

"Never too busy in this dump."

"He said something about uniforms and—"

"*Mister* Taylor! Can you beat that!" Gloria was off again. "Hey!" she directed her voice into the back of the diner, "*Mister* Taylor!" she called.

"You shut up!" came the reply.

"I only ast," she said, obviously enjoying herself. "Whadja say this girl's name was?"

"Ask her yourself. I don't know what she is. She starts Monday and she better be here on time."

"You're awful quiet," said Gloria, looking at Marcia directly for the first time.

"I only—," Marcia began.

"What's your name?"

"Kimberly," said Marcia suddenly. "I mean my name is really Marcia but everybody calls me Kimberly."

"Okay, Kim," said Gloria. "You and me are going to be real friends, see? And we'll help each other out, see? Now this here's a deep fry. Ever see a deep fry?" Gloria showed Marcia the griddle, the place where the Fry-Max cooking oil was drained of bits and then reused, the garbage, the silverware, and the uniforms. Each time she showed her something new, she popped her gum and called Marcia Kim. Marcia left after it was over, wondering what Mother would think of a person like Gloria. Then she remembered about Raymond. She hoped she could get out of the house Friday night without asking him in and going through introductions.

Marcia said the name *Kimberly* over and over again to herself. Kimberly rolled off the tongue like a lozenge. It put her in mind of a thin and perfect girl. Someone who never worried and appeared on the decks of cabin cruisers in magazine pictures, confident, holding an iced drink, and surrounded by equally attractive admirers. I'll be Kimberly from now on, Marcia thought. I'll be Kimberly and lose a lot of weight and be a whole different person. She was excited about working in the real world. She resolved at that moment to take down all the old David Cassidy posters. It was long past time. She would even take down the photograph of Jacqueline Kennedy Onassis in her wedding dress. Only the photo on her bedtable, of her mother unexplainably surrounded by baskets of apples, would remain.

"What kind of a party?" Mother asked.

"I don't know. Just a party-party."

"Who's going to be there?"

"Well, Raymond, of course, and I guess that whole group, Sue and Penny and . . ."

"Susan Sturgiss?"

"Yes, and Penny Loomis. They're both cheerleaders, and . . ." Chrissy, who had been pretending not to listen, groaned elaborately. Marcia gave her an awful look, but Chrissy had already gone back to her book. "All right," Mother said, "but I hope Raymond whoever-he-is, I hope you'll bring him in to meet your father and me before you go."

The roar of Raymond's green Harley-Davidson in the driveway elicited another sharp groan from Chrissy; then she disappeared just in time not to have to say hello. Raymond waited outside, however, revving his engine and allowing the noise to announce his presence. Marcia was able to persuade Mother that she just couldn't bring him in now. She would promise, *promise* to do it next time.

"Let her go. Let her go," said Marcia's father wearily as he finished his coffee. "I know his father. That's Siroken's boy. His father owns the Gulf station next to the bridge."

"I'm aware of that," said Mother, but she didn't insist further. She did give him a "she's *your* daughter" look that did not escape Marcia.

Marcia climbed onto the back of Raymond's motorcycle and they set off without a word. She thought she saw Chrissy looking through the upstairs hall window before they turned the corner, but she couldn't be sure.

Marcia was determined to act calm and unobtrusive among Raymond's friends. She hushed her nervousness by telling herself she was lucky to be a quiet person. Chrissy—or even Carol —would make a fool of herself in this crowd. Either of them would talk too much. Marcia was content to observe and to sit on the periphery of a group by the side of the pool. She watched carefully the way the girls, particularly Sue and

Penny, teased their boyfriends, how they kept their hair dry during a single, unhurried lap across the pool. She felt a little breathless at the easy way they accepted her now that she was with Raymond. Whatever intimacy Raymond shared with these people spun an invisible web around Marcia, and although she saw them in school every day of the year, she knew she had been transformed to them—and to herself too. She watched herself talking to them, gossiping about teachers, people in town, just the way she talked with Carol or anyone ordinary. But the difference was the nearly tipsy effulgence she felt, that made her wish the evening would never end. She was grateful her bathing suit was as brief a bikini as could be found in Gloucester, notwithstanding Mother's objections. Grateful that her hair was all right, that her figure was not too bad despite the extra ten pounds she intended to lose. Grateful, most of all, that she was a listener and, having committed to memory more than she realized she had in the past, that she knew when to laugh and make even these people believe she liked them. Marcia felt privileged to be there, almost as if she were among movie stars.

So now it's going to happen to me, she thought suddenly when Raymond came up behind her from the darkness away from the pool. He had been watching several boys as they guzzled beer after beer, piling the cans in a pyramid and then trying to jump over it. Raymond took her hand and led her through the shrubbery, up the wooden stairs of the porch, and into the house.

"Having a good time?" he asked pleasantly.

"Super," said Marcia. This was one of the first times he had spoken to her all evening. He indicated to her that she should go upstairs. Marcia knew there were bedrooms up there. Jimmy Goslau's house was legendary. It had been built around the turn of the century for what must have been an enormous family. It was reputed to have at least fifteen or twenty bedrooms on its second and third floors. Sue Sturgis had told Marcia that it was considered one of the best places in town to have a party. Mr. and Mrs. Goslau were almost always out in the evenings. A Mrs. Roberts, who drank herself to sleep every night no later than nine, was left in the maid's room as a chaperone.

"I was hoping you'd come in for a swim," Marcia said conversationally.

Raymond closed the bedroom door and stripped off his motorcycle jacket. It fell as heavily to the floor as a piece of iron. "I don't go for that stuff—swimming," he said. "At least in a pool. I like the ocean better. Swimming is for kids," Raymond added.

I mustn't make a mistake, Marcia told herself. I mustn't make a fool of myself, or the whole bunch of them will probably hear about it. Marcia was aware of the sexy reputations girls like Penny and Sue had all over the school, so when Raymond matter-of-factly took the top of her bathing suit off, she didn't protest.

She didn't protest when Raymond covered her mouth violently with his own, although it reminded her of some dreadful, sucking sea creature. And she lay back meekly when he pushed her down on the bed and climbed on top of her. Raymond had not taken off any of his clothes, and his silver Rough Rider's belt buckle felt cold and hard against her bare stomach. God, he must weigh over 200 pounds, Marcia told herself. She tried to balance his torso between her thighs.

"What the hell are you doing?" Raymond asked suddenly.

Marcia looked up wretchedly at him. "I . . . uh . . . ."

"Jesus! Nobody told me you were that fast!" he said. "Who'd you go with before? You didn't go with anybody, did you?"

"Well, no, but—"

"What are you trying to do?"

"Trying to *do*? I . . . well, I didn't think I was doing *any-thing*. I was just . . ." Marcia's words trailed off. Carol's older sister had let Carol and Marcia look through her marriage manual. The woman described in the book had done a great many things, none of which Marcia would have dared try. Marcia had just lain there underneath him, hoping it would be over, hoping he would stop, and now . . . Misery, she told herself. I've done something awful and I don't even know what it is!

"I used to go with a girl like you once," Raymond said, pleasant again. He grinned. "She was just, almost like you."

"Like me?" Marcia asked, hoping to stall off another of his vacuum-cleaner-like assaults on her mouth.

"Yeah. She was . . . she didn't know much either, but she came around pretty soon. She loved it. But you're just putting me on, being so fast and all, aren't you?"

"I didn't know I was being fast," Marcia managed to say.

Raymond pulled an exaggerated "far-be-it-from-me" face. "Listen! Who's complaining?" he said. "Not me! I just thought you being kind of young and all I wouldn't go all the way, but if you want it, I've got it, baby."

Miserably, Marcia endured the buzz-saw motion of Raymond on top of her. He was so heavy he took her breath away, and his beard rubbed her face raw. She prayed for just a space of air between herself and Raymond to catch her breath. She prayed Mrs. Roberts downstairs would wake up. Maybe the Goslaus would come home. Raymond worked over her breasts as if he were trying to restore a heartbeat, and she knew she should push him away just on principle, but she wanted more than anything to say no to his heaviness, his beard, his frighten-ing her. When at last he sat up, he said, "What's the matter?"

"Nothing. I . . . ."

"Well, you need some experience, that's all," he said, and lit a cigarette. "I thought you were . . . kind of young, all along."

"I guess so. I mean . . . I don't know what I mean," she said unhappily.

"There's two kinds of women in this world," Raymond said, his cigarette between his teeth. Marcia noticed he didn't inhale any smoke. "Whores," he continued, "and, well, like nuns, like. You were kidding me, making me think you were the first kind. But that's okay. You don't have to be a nun for the rest of your life. You just need a little experience, that's all. Like this girl I was telling you about. Where I used to live. It was the first time she'd ever done it . . . with me. I was her first. She loved it."

Raymond had been new in school last year. He had taken his place at the top of this superior group of juniors and seniors effortlessly from whatever place he had lived in and gone to school before. But what confidence Marcia had felt in the early evening drained from her when she realized he didn't seem as familiar and safe as the other Gloucester High kids. Not that Jimmy Goslau and his friends were *that* safe looking, it was just that they'd been in her classes since the eighth grade, and she was not sure, suddenly, who Raymond was. He acted almost like an adult, she thought, someone who could drift in and out of town. She tried to picture the other girl, a faraway double, enjoying this, loving this. Not enjoying this, Marcia said to herself, not if she's really anything like me at all. She wondered how Raymond could know who was like her and who was not, but all she could think to say was, "You mean she had blond hair and everything?"

"Everything," Raymond repeated. "Now just relax and light my fire, baby."

"I . . . please . . . I don't want to go all the way," she said. "I'm afraid, Raymond."

"Nothing to be afraid of," Raymond said, chuckling. He

pulled out his wallet and from it took a little foil package and waved it in front of her. It looked quite worn. Marcia didn't dare ask about it. If she said something stupid, she was sure it would get out and everyone would know and laugh at her. She thought ruefully of the fantasies that had kept her awake nights. This was nothing like what she'd imagined at all. She didn't know what she would do do if he took his "thing" out. If his beard and his hands were that rough and hurtful, the "other"—she couldn't bring herself to think the word—would probably be excruciating, but she was too afraid to say no. Maybe he wouldn't. Maybe he just wouldn't. Maybe she could stop him if he did.

Marcia lay back down underneath him. Perhaps she and this other girl shared some dreadful infirmity she knew nothing about. After a while, Raymond simply sat up with an exasperated sigh. She guessed that it was all right to put the top of her bathing suit back on.

He was angry. She could tell by his silence and the position in which he lay smoking a cigarette on the bed. He watched as she combed her hair in front of the mirror in the full moonlight. Marcia didn't really want to fix her hair in front of Raymond; on the other hand she didn't want to go downstairs looking messy. She thought of the other girls at the party, how they had emerged, tangle-haired, from bedrooms and dark places in the house and grounds at different times during the evening. There was a keen satisfaction on their faces as they took note of who was watching them.

Marcia sensed that the whole business of sex was not really completed until it had been discussed a little. Whatever it was you did with a boy had to be giggled over and exaggerated to not-so-close friends, perhaps talked about worriedly and honestly with one best friend, and made known through just the right channels to just the right hazy extent. She missed

Carol. It seemed that even in this crowd, the friend couples among the girls were as important and more permanent than the boy-girl couples.

Marcia knew one thing from the marriage manual she had read with Carol, however. Although she had allowed Raymond to do pretty much as he pleased with her, he was angry, and this was her fault.

Marcia had expected Mother to make her life miserable over the job at Taylor's diner, but curiously she didn't. She even seemed to enjoy the gossip Marcia brought home in the afternoons. The only thing Mother objected to was the food.

"At least have a good breakfast," Mother insisted many times. "I don't know what you get to eat in a place like that but if you want to lose weight and clear up your face, you might think about how much fat they use."

But Marcia always had breakfast at Taylor's. Every morning but Sunday she woke a minute before her alarm clock buzzed. She made her bed and was out of the house by five-thirty, long before anyone had stirred. Not touching a thing in the silent kitchen, she closed the screen door softly behind her, as if to preserve without interruption the first little world of her own.

She never had to eat eggs or cereal and enjoyed the eerie silence of having breakfast with Mr. Taylor before the day's first customers came in. She relished the dripping hash-brown potatoes, and dipped her donut in the scalding, black coffee, just as he did. She stared pleasantly at him across the big old wooden table in the diner's kitchen. Sometimes Mr. Taylor acknowledged her presence with only a grunt and didn't bother to look up, but as the summer went on, he became more talkative and even allowed how things were better now that Gloria didn't have the early shift. One time he admitted to Marcia that he thought her surprisingly prompt and polite for a high school girl. Then he added bitterly that it wouldn't last long. She'd grow up and learn to be "like all the rest." At first Marcia felt that Mr. Taylor piled all the aggravations he had suffered at the hands of young people on her shoulders, but as he grew accustomed to her good nature he softened and even confided to Marcia that he had had a daughter too—once. "Somewhere . . . God knows what she's up to now," he said, as if this daughter were a long-divorced wife.

Marcia's favorite time was before eight in the morning. The fishermen came in and talked about the weather, and all the other early morning people who started the town going every day sat with their coffee and donuts and gossiped. Marcia loved being a part of this secret existence. She liked to imagine that she and the men in the diner were the only people up in the whole world. She enjoyed the fact that Mother and Chrissy and her teachers and even Raymond had all disappeared for a little while, all asleep and unable to touch her for these few hours a day. Sharon would laugh if she knew Marcia was getting up at five o'clock in the morning. She was not able to explain about this magic space of time to Sharon and so did not mention it in her letters.

The men treated her with a familiar, gentle humor that caused her to wonder if they too felt this was a wonderful few hours, before the day built up into its usual annoying hum. Marcia learned all their names and what they did and whether they took black or cream, whether they liked their eggs over or sunny. She liked being called Kim. She enjoyed being good and being liked. Except for Raymond, she was happy.

Marcia did feel a little powerful in Raymond's presence. She was certain that Carol and even Chrissy secretly admired his muttonchop sideburns and his noisy Harley Davidson. At times, when they were alone together, she felt like his pet, an angora kitten riding only by accidental joke on the back of his motorcycle. Raymond liked to drive around for hours. Marcia didn't mind so long as they kept off Route 1, where there were other bike riders and where he drove very fast. She did not know whether the Hell's Angels insignia on the back of his jacket, which Raymond claimed was authentic, was a joke or not.

At parties and at the beach on Sunday they were usually surrounded by Raymond's friends. Marcia did her best to act as if it were the most normal thing in the world for her to be there. She even tried to look sultry and victorious, like Penny and Sue, over the envy she could engender in the faces of those who, like Chrissy, had to go to the beach alone or with other girls, but she couldn't manage to be that cruel.

Raymond did what she assumed all boys did when they went off with their girl friends to bedrooms or spare rooms during the evening of a party. She knew the girl was supposed to give in to the boy, but just how she was supposed to give in she didn't know, since Raymond gave her no clues. One time she took off her own blouse and bra. "Trying to kid me again?" was his reaction to that. Laughingly, he had said that—almost but not quite affectionately. Once, when she felt his belt buckle pressing firmly against her, she felt her whole self light up with a numbing desire. She wanted to tell him to hold her, to touch her there, where she touched herself secretly, but he had raised his head quizzically, like a terrier listening for an intruder, intently concentrating on the sounds in the house. "Did you hear a car drive in?" he asked. "I think it's Penny's parents, damn them. We better get out of here. I don't want to get you in trouble." But it hadn't been Penny's parents or anyone at all, and Marcia was ashamed of the dark, mercurial pleasure she had felt. It probably put her in the whore category. She resolved not to allow herself to feel it again.

Once she found him gazing quite mournfully at her in a quiet moment as he lay on top of her, but he never produced the little foil package again. Marcia knew something was wrong. She tried to remember certain things her sister had said. "Men are all alike. They're all cut from the same ball of wax and they all want one thing and they want it all the time." Had Sharon been joking? Had she meant Buddy and not Moose? Sharon would have probably fit into the whore category. Marcia wanted desperately not to. She wished Raymond were not so heavy. She wished he would take his boots off when he climbed on top of her. She wished he would shave more closely. Most of all, she wished she knew what was wrong. Only once had she ever felt aroused during these sessions with Raymond. She guessed she ought to be enjoying them, but her feelings were too faint under Raymond's weight and roughness for her to hold onto them.

She assumed he would stop seeing her presently. He would get fed up and never call her again and she would go back to school in September and none of his wonderful friends would pay the slightest attention to her again. It would be as if all this had never happened and she would be back at the movies with Carol on Friday nights. She couldn't understand why he had included her in the first place. She was an ordinary outsider, not a bit like the cheerleaders, football players, class officers, editors—those people who in different ways stood out in the school. Despite his low marks, Raymond had a quality everybody called *funky,* which made even John Brogdan, editor of the school newspaper, like him and kid him about his Hell's Angels jacket. Marcia did not stand out in the school in any way. "No outstanding characteristics" was a phrase she had once come upon in a biology text. That describes me, she had thought. But to her surprise, whatever reasons Raymond had for seeing her did not run dry. He always appeared at ten-thirty in the morning at Taylor's for his coffeee break no matter how perfunctory his manner had been the night before.

Marcia wanted so much to tell Carol her worries, but Carol was fading away from her slowly. She wanted to tell Carol how furious Raymond got sometimes. How she couldn't say anything then, couldn't make it better in any way. His anger could dilate a room until she thought everything in it would explode. At other times he seemed so happy with her, when she mended a rip in his blue jeans, when he lay with his head in her lap for hours, both of them silently listening to Jimmy Goslau play his guitar. Mostly Raymond seemed delighted to have her on the back of his bike. He would turn around every once in a while and grin at her, and when she smiled back, waves of laughter would overcome him. He would not explain why. Then too, he was so very good looking. Marcia wanted to tell Carol how it made her feel to be seen with Raymond.

Carol didn't call for a whole week in August. She went shopping with other friends. Then she went away to the Cape with her family for two weeks and didn't write at all. As with Chemistry I and French II, which boggled her mind when she considered the school year ahead, Marcia supposed that she would have to push herself and make friends in Raymond's crowd, another accomplishment to keep everything evenly in its place while she worked in school so diligently and with no mind to anything but the next milestone ahead. The girls in Raymond's crowd treated her in an airy, friendly way, but clearly she had to make her own way among them. She hoped this would happen by itself. Osmosis was the word, osmosis—a word in a vocabulary test, or was it a science test?

"I never get to see you anymore," Chrissy complained one day. "You're always away from home."

"Well, I have to be at Taylor's at quarter of six in the morning," Marcia answered, "and then there's Raymie and everything."

"How much are you making?"

"Oh, about fifty a week with tips, usually."

"Gee, I only make twenty."

"I know," said Marcia. "But just think, you're giving lessons and stuff. I couldn't give any kind of lessons if I wanted to."

Chrissy picked at a spot of manure on her new, high riding boots. She had bought them with her own money, and Marcia knew they were the fulfillment of a lifelong dream. Still, she couldn't bring herself to compliment anything as outlandish as riding boots. "You could give lessons if you wanted," Chrissy said thoughtfully. "You could go over to Revere and teach remedial reading in their summer program in the slums."

Marcia shrugged. "That sounds like another one of Mother's ideas," she said.

"Well, it is. But I was thinking of doing it."

"How much does it pay?"

"Pay? It doesn't pay anything. You just do it, you know, to help and all."

"Oh. Well, I guess I don't have time now. Maybe next summer."

Chrissy sat on Sharon's bed, which had mysteriously remained in the room since Sharon's last tumultuous visit. She had brought a tin of Goddard's English Boot Wax with her and began to polish her boots lovingly. "If you don't keep the leather soft, it'll dry up on you," she said.

As usual, Marcia didn't quite know what to say to Chrissy. She decided to set her hair.

"What happened to all those things you used to have on your bulletin board, those posters?"

"Oh, I took 'em down. They were old. They got dusty."

Chrissy settled into a cross-legged position. "I don't see Carol around much. What's the matter? Don't you guys like each other anymore?"

"Carol? She's on vacation. They go to the Cape. Wellfleet or someplace."

"Hey, Marsh?"

"What?"

"What do you do with Raymond?"

"What do you mean, what do I do?"

"You know. I mean like what everybody says that crowd does at parties and all."

"We sit around. Some kids smoke pot. I don't know. We listen to music mostly, talk and everything. I don't know."

"Yes, but I mean . . . well, do you like him a whole lot?"

"He's okay."

"Well, you see an awful lot of him if you don't like him that much."

"I do like him. He's neat."

Chrissy paused in her polishing to hold her boot up to the light. Then she continued in the very same spot. "You know what Mom thinks," she said.

"I can imagine. But she's wrong."

"You mean you're still a virgin and all?"

"Yep." Marcia did not turn around but kept winding her hair tightly around her electric rollers.

"Mom says she's worried you're going to get pregnant like Sharon. She says Mrs. Albert told her all the kids in that crowd sleep with each other. Is that true?"

"I don't know. Why don't you ask them?"

"But you must know *something!* I mean you're *there.*"

"Nope."

"Do you have anything, like I mean pills or anything?"

"Nope."

Chrissy polished vigorously. "Gee, you're communicative today," she said.

Marcia thought she would let that remark go. Then she surprised herself and said, "You know, Chrissy, you have a really bad habit, just like Mother."

"What do you mean by that?"

"Well, you sound just like Mother, accusing me of getting pregnant, which I'm not so stupid as to do, and then you act like you never said it." Marcia stopped for breath. "And then you ask some dumb question and make me forget why I'm angry but I'm still mad."

Chrissy took another gob of wax out of the can. Her lower lip stuck out so that Marcia could not tell whether she was sorry or angry. She seemed to digest this for many minutes, then she said, "You're right."

Marcia wanted to say, "That's okay," but she knew it would happen again.

"I guess I'm an awful lot like Mom. I know Mom is uptight about anything to do with sex. Do you think I'm going to grow up and be that way too?"

Marcia laughed.

"Why are you laughing? I'm serious."

"I don't know why I'm laughing. I'm sorry. It's such a funny question, that's all."

"Well, they talk about things like that in psych books. 'The sins of the fathers.' "

"What?"

"The sins of the fathers are visited upon the sons. That's

in the Bible. It means, well . . . that things get passed along."

"Since when are you reading psych books and the Bible?"

Chrissy studied her boot in the light. She turned it around critically and started rubbing the toe with the bottom of a water tumbler. "I'm reading psych to be prepared for freshman psych at Yale. I've decided I'm going to go there," she said. "And I'm not reading the Bible. That's just an expression from the Bible everybody knows."

Everybody but poor dumb me, Marcia thought. "So you're going to be a psychiatrist or something now?" she asked.

"Yep. That or maybe an anthropologist."

"I thought Yale was for boys."

"Gee, you're out of it. They started accepting girls ages ago. Didn't you hear?"

Marcia sighed as she finished the last roller. "Well, it sounds like a great place to be a girl," she said.

Chrissy snorted. "I suppose if you look at it that way, but you really ought to start thinking about your career, Marsh."

"You sound just like Mother again."

"All right, so what? She's right about a lot of things. She said to me she would have had a career herself except that when she was in school women just graduated and got married. I'm certainly not going to waste my life getting married and having kids."

"How come you always want to know so much about sex, then?"

"I don't want to know. You're the one who's always talking about it."

"Chris, that isn't true and you know it."

"It is so. You're always talking about it. You must have sex on the brain or something, but you better watch it because you can get into trouble."

"You're full of a lot of suggestions for me, Chris," said Marcia. "Believe it or not, I've got one for you."

"What? Find some boyfriend with a motorcycle because you think I'm so frustrated or something?"

"What's wrong with Raymond's bike?"

"It pollutes the environment, for one thing."

"Pollutes the environment!"

"It does, and it's a noise pollution agent too."

"So find yourself someone who'll take you out on a horse like they used to in 1492. I don't know."

"I didn't mean to criticize Raymond. I just meant you should start thinking of yourself as an entity apart from some man's reflection."

"What's that supposed to mean?" Marcia asked patiently.

"Oh, that whole bunch of kids . . . the boys treat the girls like they were toys, sex symbols. God! They're still going steady with each other and exchanging I.D. bracelets and all that teen-age stuff that went out years ago. A bunch of pussy-cats and male chauvinist pigs. They all think they're so wonderful in high school, but when they graduate they just get married and pregnant and go to work for the telephone company or something. It all ends with high school. Believe me. A cute little wedding and then *bang!* a life of dishes."

"You still didn't listen to my suggestion, Chris."

"What is it then?"

"Stop being so jealous. Learn how to put on makeup and dress and do your hair and stuff. Anybody can do it. Just read *Seventeen* magazine. You look like a boy half the time."

The water tumbler smashed against the wall. Marcia gaped at the little black crescent it made in the plaster and then at the littered glass on the floor.

"You're going to be sorry you ever said that," Chrissy

whispered. Her face was crimson, but her expression so worked its way around her face that it all blurred to Marcia.

"I'm sorry. I'm really sorry . . . I . . . "

"I'm telling Mom what you do with Raymond."

"What do you know about Raymond?"

"I heard what happened last Friday night. You went into a bedroom with him at Sturgiss's party. I heard they all call you Kim too."

"Who told you that?"

"Never mind who told me. I'm telling Mom."

"Go and tell her. It's a lie anyway." Marcia spun around to face the mirror. She didn't care. Nothing had happened. She would just deny everything.

"Boy! Talk about lying in wait and twisting the knife." Chrissy actually stamped. "You're the champ!"

"I'm sorry. I didn't mean it. It just came out that way."

"I'm sorry, I didn't mean it. It just came out that way," Chrissy mimicked.

"Well, you didn't have to say that about the telephone company."

"What about the telephone company?"

Marcia shook her head slowly. "You see what I mean? You know perfectly well my sister works for the phone company. Why do you have to be so mean about Sharon?"

"I forgot. I wasn't even *thinking* about your stupid sister."

"Don't call her stupid either."

Chrissy had stepped on a piece of glass. She sat on the bed and jammed her big toe in her mouth. Marcia started picking up the larger pieces. She was afraid of broken glass. She heard Chrissy crying but she didn't want to look.

"I swear this family's like an armed camp," Chrissy muttered, rocking back and forth holding her foot. Marcia said nothing but continued to pick up the glass bit by bit, squinting to see the slivers in the light.

"I'm not saying it's all your fault. You just didn't have to say that about my looking like a boy!"

"I didn't mean to hurt your feelings."

"There are a hundred ways of helping someone without humiliating them."

"And that's what you do, Chrissy, right?"

"I never humiliated you."

"Oh, no?"

Chrissy got up and limped to the door. "Just wait till College Boards, that's all!" she shot back over her shoulder.

Marcia was kneeling on the carpet, still collecting glass. She looked up in astonishment. "I did pretty well in the practice ones," she said.

"Five hundreds!"

"That's pretty good, I thought. You didn't do much better."

"I did too, if you want to know. Mom made me say I had six hundreds just so *you* wouldn't feel bad. I got 780 English and 750 math."

Marcia's fingers tightened on a piece of glass. She had to wait this moment out without having any reaction. Then she could think about it later on. It wouldn't matter so much. Her teachers had told her 500 was a good score. They had all said so.

"I'm in the ninety-eighth percentile too, nationwide. How about you?" Chrissy said and slammed the door behind herself.

Marcia sat down in her chair, a little pile of glass still winking in her hand. The room itself seemed to relax around her. No one had ever mentioned a percentile to her, although she would have gladly settled for the ninety-seventh or even the seventy-ninth. She supposed that whoever decided on percentiles was only really interested in the ninety-eighth anyway and hadn't bothered to make up other ones for people like her.

· II ·

> It isn't unlikely that these mutations were not caused by the amount of protein in the DNA molecule in the foxes of the Y control group, but by the nature of the RNA molecule itself. However, later experiments with the same group of silver foxes proved to the contrary, and Morgan, whose experiments with the common fruit fly preceded Crick and Watson by nearly half a century, could not have but concurred.

It's all here, Marcia told herself. Somewhere in the first paragraph maybe? She closed one eye and tried to cross out one of the nots in her mind. Two nots give me a positive, one more means a negative. Isn't unlikely. Not caused. That means it isn't unlikely, *is* unlikely, drop the second not, so these mutations *were* caused by the amount of protein, not the RNA molecule . . . so it's *not* caused by the amount of protein. If only I were allowed to use my pencil to cross out a couple of nots, Marcia wished. She looked around at the cafeteria walls. They had been stripped of all announcements and posters, as if someone had thought that a notice for the Red Cross drive or a basketball pep rally might give away an answer or intrude on the gravity of the Scholastic Aptitude Examinations. From where Marcia was sitting, she could just see Chrissy's back at the front of the room. She appeared to be writing very fast. Perhaps she had got past the Mutations of Silver Foxes and the other reading comprehension passages and was already on the vocabulary. Marcia considered skipping ahead. She had been well drilled in vocabulary. She swallowed three Tums and went on to the next passage, which happened to be South American History.

The attempted raid on Bolivian headquarters would not have occurred had the Spanish been informed of the lack of

A. hemp
B. tin and molybdenum
C. naval stores
D. none of the above

Marcia decided it was time for a "none of the above." Billy Vinculli, in the seat directly ahead of her, was drumming his pencil annoyingly. When he leaned forward, Marcia could see the top of his jockey briefs over the edge of his pants, the same kind Raymond wore. She had seen Raymond's underwear in a pile once, at the beach, after they had come in from swimming. Boys' underwear was disgusting, but a little exciting too, unlike her father's baggy old boxer shorts. Marcia tried to picture Raymond in boxer shorts and executive length socks. Impossible. Some sort of wear and tear had removed most of the hair from her father's legs over the years, perhaps it was those executive length socks. Raymond's legs were hairy and tan. Once she had glanced over and seen right through the open leg of his bathing trunks to what was inside. She had averted her eyes immediately, but the memory was vivid. She had just decided to come back to the essays later when she discovered that her eyes were filled with tears. She had been staring uncomprehendingly at the paragraph before her for several minutes and, because she hadn't the faintest idea what it was about, was completely unable to answer a single question. Some awful person, a teacher, no doubt, seemed to be yelling the garbled language of the essay in her ear. *It's so easy. Why can't you do it? Why can't you do it? Stupid! Stupid! Concentrate. You're thinking about Raymond instead. Stupid Marcia can't even answer a simple question!*

Marcia had run out of Tums. She debated taking her second roll up to Mr. McElvain, the proctor, and letting him go through it to make sure there were no notes on any of the tablets or on the wrapper, but she decided that would take too much time.

> A series of poems might be composed of two sorts. In the one, the incidents and agents were to be, in part at least, supernatural; and the excellence aimed at was to consist in the interesting of the affections by the dramatic truth of such emotions, as would naturally accompany such situations, supposing them real in this sense. And real they have been in this sense to every human being, in every village and town, who, from whatever source of delusion, has at any time believed himself under supernatural agency.

Marcia read the passage four times. She knew immediately that the agents and agency referred to had nothing to do with spies. That was too easy, and since it was not mentioned in any of the questions she discarded the idea, although it would have made her a fraction more interested in what she was reading.

What . . . what on earth was that supposed to mean? She heard herself asking the same question Raymond had asked after he flipped through the English part of her study booklet that weekend. He claimed that none of the passages made any sense at all. Marcia was afraid to agree with him because she knew if she let down her guard for even an instant and admitted how the reading bored her, sealed off her mind and all her senses—save one little opening through which she allowed the printed words to trickle like a Chinese water torture—she would be lost and unable to study at all. Marcia had stayed up until one o'clock the night before the test. First Raymond, who was not bothering to take

SATs, and then her father quizzed her on the vocabulary section. Raymond had been unable to pronounce a great many of the words, Marcia had noticed. She had gone through her Monarch Notes, and reread all of Lamb's *Tales from Shakespeare*, although Chrissy had turned up her nose at condensations of any kind. Chrissy was amazing. She read everything only in the original and did not study very much for the exam.

> In a certain office, $\frac{1}{3}$ of the workers are women, $\frac{1}{2}$ of the women are married and $\frac{1}{3}$ of the married women have children. If $\frac{3}{4}$ of the men are married and $\frac{2}{3}$ of the men have children, what part of the workers are without children?

Math was better. Math was safe. At least it didn't hide things from her in tricky configurations of words. If only they allowed her figuring space to work out the English questions in the same way. Math and science could at least be studied ahead of time with some fair assurance of progress. Perhaps if her math was good enough she wouldn't have to worry about English. Maybe there were colleges that accepted people who were good in the sciences and didn't expect them to take English at all.

Someone had carved a crude picture of a pregnant woman in the desk, filled the lines in with ink, and labeled it "Rita." Marcia had been tracing the drawing idly for several moments when she thought of Sharon—pregnant now. Buddy was back from Vietnam unharmed. "We're calling him Anthony Jr.," she had written in her last letter, as though there were no possibility of the baby's being a girl. Sharon had sent a picture of herself in a maternity smock, sideways, grinning at a grinning Buddy, who was doing a handstand on the arm of a chair. The chair had been placed so that Buddy would appear to be doing a handstand on Sharon's protruding stomach. Marcia shuddered. She went up to Mr. McElvain and placed the roll of Tums before him, but he waved her away with a smile and didn't bother to inspect them.

"How do you think you did?"

"Terrible. I know I did worse than last year. I know it!" Chrissy moaned, but Chrissy always said she did badly on a test and then when the results came in, she invariably got an A.

"What did you get on the first one, the first question on the silver foxes?"

"B."

"B! I thought it was D!" Marcia gasped, sure that Chrissy must be right because she was Chrissy.

"No. There was a triple negative in there—isn't, unlikely, and were not, I think. It was tricky, but what you do is ignore the first two, which cancel each other out, and read the third one. Cinch. The math was tough though. The math was very tough."

Marcia closed her eyes against the memory of the test, but she found herself saying, "Why is it . . . why can't they just write things the way people talk? Well, maybe a little better than the way people talk, but at least so you can understand what they mean?"

"Oh, I don't know," said Chrissy. "I rather agree with their point of view. At least I can understand their problem. If they wrote it so just anybody could understand it, they wouldn't be able to find out how smart you were."

"They'll find out in a hurry about me," said Marcia.

"Not necessarily. Everybody thinks they've failed, always. But if you get something like a seventy out of all the questions, I think you'll be fine, about 680 or so. You have to remember that half the people they test all over the country are complete idiots."

How pleasant it was not to be included in Chrissy's group of idiots, Marcia told herself. She wondered when that had happened. Raymond however, the non-SAT taker, the non-college-bound motorcyclist, would definitely fall into this category. And if Chrissy had suspected just how stupid Marcia knew herself to be, Chrissy would have included her as well.

"Well, I have to go now," said Marcia. "I'm not going home."

"Where are you going?"

"I'm meeting Raymie and the kids at the drugstore."

"Oh. Well, to each his own."

"See you."

"Sure."

There was such envy in Chrissy's voice. Marcia watched her walk slowly down the street, swinging her battered Navajo pocketbook in a circle until the strap got twisted, then swinging it the other way. Chrissy would go for a ride now, Marcia supposed. She always took a ride after anything tense, an argument, a test, a prod from Mother about her hair. One time she and Raymond had caught a glimpse of Chrissy from the car window. She had been galloping on Morris almost angrily through the hushed snowy woods beside the highway, oblivious to the sagging branches that shed snow in her face when she hit them and to the logs that poked out of the slush in the path before her.

"Who does she think she is? Roy Rogers?" Raymond had asked.

Chrissy would be all right, Marcia decided, if she'd be a little less conceited, if she would set her hair instead of letting it hang in a curly mess. Chrissy had very nice hair really, and if she was as thin as a rail, well, she could wear tight sweaters and pants and show off her figure. But Chrissy wore straight tweed skirts and flowered blouses to school. Marcia could never quite believe it, but Marcia never mentioned these thoughts to Chrissy again after their last argument. Chrissy absolutely could not make herself attractive. She wouldn't dare even try. That was her terrible secret. On the other hand, Chrissy would sure as anything get into Yale, early admission she said she wanted, and she would be a liberated woman and an anthropologist, or what was it?— a historical novelist she wanted to be now? Or was that what Mother wanted Chrissy to be and Chrissy didn't want to be? As for Marcia, Mother didn't seem to care, beyond getting into college, beyond being unlike that photograph of Sharon.

"So why do you let her get to you like that?"

"I don't know, Raymie. Usually I don't, but tonight at dinner she said something horrible."

"What did she say?"

"She said she expected Chris to get near enough to eight hundred so she wouldn't have to take them again next year, and me to get at least middle six hundreds."

Raymond slowed the car and turned into a dead-end road that led down to the beach. "So?" he asked.

"So she . . . it's like Chrissy and I were things in one of her collections, like those African animal statues she collects, and Chrissy's the most valuable thing in it and me, I'm nothing, and she actually thinks she's being nice and encouraging and all the time she makes me feel stupider and stupider. Even when my marks go up I can't help feeling dumb all the time because I have to keep working harder and harder and Chris never works at all. Like French. Chrissy actually *speaks* French. She does it all the time with Jennie. They do it in front of me so I won't understand and they even do it on the bus and in public in loud voices and they think it's a big joke and people are going to think they're French or something. It's all I can do to memorize the conjugations. I can't understand a word Mlle Ramon says."

"But I thought you did fine in French."

"I do. I got a B plus. But last week I just could have *died*. I wanted to go to . . . the girls' room and everything, and we aren't allowed to say anything in class in English, and it took me ten minutes to get it out right even though I'd written it down and looked up the words. Everybody laughed. And there was Chrissy, laughing like a hyena."

"Well, maybe they were just laughing in sympathy like," Raymond said. "It could happen to anybody. You should try to get up in front of the class with a hard-on, if you think that's bad."

Marcia hesitated. She was not sure what he meant. "Some of them weren't laughing in sympathy," she said.

Raymond stopped the car at the beach in front of a chain that swung idly between two posts. "But if I'd been there, I mean I might have cracked up too, you know, and you'd know I wasn't trying to be mean or anything. Lemme tell you, I couldn't get through this year if you didn't help me with French and that MacBeth thing. You're so tough on yourself, Kim. You always think people are laughing at you, thinking you're stupid . . . people *like* you. Everybody likes you . . . you . . ."

"Chrissy thinks I'm stupid."

"So how's her love life?"

"Pretty bad, I guess."

"And how's your love life?"

"Okay, I guess," Marcia said. She turned away from him self-consciously. She didn't want him to start in just yet. "I just wish things wouldn't get to me so much, Raymie," she said. "I never used to be that way."

"You let them push you around."

"No, I don't. Not really. But the thing is they're right, you know. Even Daddy goes along with it now. If I want to go to college, I'll have to keep working like this. I have to keep killing myself. They say how Shar is living a zero life and I shouldn't grow up to be like that, and in a way they're right, Raymie, because in her last letter she acts like she's going to have a boy, and I mean she's . . . what's Buddy going to do if it's a girl? It isn't Sharon's fault. She doesn't sound very happy deep down, and I *don't* want to be like that, but still, I hate school and if I have to work like this for four more years in college I think I'll just die. My eyes will stop working. My head will stop working like . . . like an old car."

Raymond laughed. Marcia closed her eyes. She felt his arm solidly around the back of her shoulders. She put her head against his chest and sighed.

"You don't seem much like an old car to me," Raymond said. "As a matter of fact, you remind me of a new Pantera."

"What's a Pantera?"

"It's a neat Italian sportscar. You don't see hardly any of them. They cost fifteen grand. Jimmy was going to get one when he graduates. His old man was going to pay, but Jimmy couldn't wait. He got that Vette, the dope."

"Why is he a dope?" Marcia asked sleepily.

"They're badly engineered. A Pantera is a . . . a work of art," he said reverently.

"Is that the kind of car you're going to sell, Raymie?"

"Nah. I couldn't get a franchise if I tried."

"What's the car then?"

"Mercedes. I told you."

"I'm sorry. I forgot."

"That's okay. Girls don't know anything about cars. It's a good car though, a beautiful car."

Marcia nodded absently. Raymond believed in cars, in engines. Marcia did not know very much about mechanics, but she did understand the respect he had for something tangible, something he could take apart with his hands and actually see. At least that made some sense. Words in books, in the air, were not to be trusted. "Anthropologist"—what did that mean? Probably somebody who learned a whole bunch of excruciatingly difficult stuff and then just went and taught it to other people who would, in turn, teach it to yet more people, like a relay race of jugglers, juggling words instead of pins, never letting them touch the ground.

"What are you thinking?"

"Oh, nothing. Just thinking."

"You think too much," he said and smiled, predictably pushing her down on the front seat of the car. Marcia could see Raymond's teeth in the reflected moonlight. The lower ones were bent in. She wondered if he ever went to a dentist, if his parents cared or had the money. She began to imagine him in a dentist's chair. She could picture the bile green and chrome drill, its monstrous base bolted to the floor, and all the pain and power in that base transferred perfectly into a series of ever-diminishing arms, ending in a furious speck in Raymond's mouth. She joined her fingers lightly on his back and held herself in disguised rigidity for as long as she could.

He liked undressing her—that much she knew. She allowed him to open her blouse and take off her bra and put his hands on her breasts. She listened to the sound of his boots scraping against the inside of the door. She worried he would damage the leather. Now that it was too cold for the motorcycle, Raymond borrowed a car from his father's repair service every time they went out. Whether he told his father or not she didn't know, but he usually didn't pick an expensive one like this. Somebody else owned this Lincoln Continental. Somebody had left a gray kid glove in the front seat. It was a man's glove. Marcia had never seen a man wear gray kid gloves.

"Where are you?" Raymond asked suddenly.

"What? I'm right here."

"No you're not."

"Yes, I'm here. What do you mean?"

"You're dreaming. You're not thinking about me. What is it? That dumb test?"

"No, it isn't, Raymie. I just . . . I'm sorry."

"Jesus!"

"Raymie, what do you want me to do? Why is it that . . . ? This is supposed to be fun and everything. What am I doing wrong? Just *tell* me."

"Turn me on! Do something, baby . . . Jesus H. Christ!"

"Well I . . . I want to . . . to . . . you know. I mean . . . oh, Raymie, if you'd let me have a little time to sort of . . . Once I felt like if only you'd put . . . your hand . . ."

"If only *I!* If only *I!*" he said. "You're telling *me* what to do! Every time I think you're going to say okay, you freeze up! Just when I'm getting real excited you make like a nutcracker. Do you know what a cock teaser is? Well, you're a cock teaser! That's what you are. Any other guy in his right mind would have dropped you long ago."

"Oh, Raymie, I'm so sorry. Please just tell me what you want me to do. Please."

"What the hell," said Raymond. "Forget it. Maybe we should stop seeing each other." He sat with one foot crooked in the steering wheel, staring out at the ocean.

"Raymie?"

"What."

"Please don't be mad."

"I'm not mad."

"Yes, you are. Won't you . . . can't we talk about this?"

"Okay," he snapped. "All you do is lie there. *Lie* there. You don't do a damn thing."

"Well, should I . . . do you want me to . . . well, put my hand . . . I mean . . . you know what I mean."

"You could, for a change."

"Well, I thought so. But I tried that one time. Do you remember? Last summer—I think it was at Penny's house and you pushed my hand away and you got angry?"

"No, I don't remember."

"But it's true, Raymie. You don't seem to want me to . . . to even touch you. I mean *there*."

"Sure, sure. That's why I put my arm around you. That's why I lay down on top of you. Because I don't want you to touch me. Got any other bright ideas?"

"I don't know, Raymie. I just thought if we talked about it a little we could—"

"Talking! That's all you want to do."

"But I . . . Are you trying to tell me that if, like . . . well if I really liked it and all, it'd be better for you? Because if that *is* what you're saying, then . . . well, I was just thinking if you were a little gentler and everything and didn't make me feel like you were rushing me and all, I might . . ."

"Boy, you've got a lot to learn."

"Raymie?"

"What."

"Could you tell me just one thing?"

"What."

"Remember when I was telling you about French class and you said the word . . . hard-on, I think it was? Well, I'm not going to ask you what that is, because I think I know, but is . . . is that supposed to happen when you"—Marcia swallowed hard—"you know, kind of . . . when we are, like, in the car or up in somebody's room?"

Raymond stamped out his cigarette on the floor of the car. He didn't answer. He jammed the key into the ignition.

"Because if it is . . . supposed to happen . . . I mean does it? To you? I think I'd feel it . . . I mean maybe if it isn't happening that's what's wrong."

Raymond backed up the car and wheeled it viciously out onto the highway. "You keep your cotton-pickin' hands to yourself," he said, practically through clenched teeth. "And you keep your mind out of the gutter and think about why you're . . . frigid," he said after thinking about the word *frigid* for a minute.

"Raymie, *please* don't go so fast."

"Now you're telling me how to drive too!"

"I'm not. You scare me so. Please!"

"Talk talk."

"But talking helps sometimes. I know it's awful to talk about, but . . . "

"All you have to know is one thing," said Raymond, accelerating even more. "I'm not getting anything out of you, baby."

"Well, why do you take me out then? Why don't you go out with Penny or Sue? Why take stupid old me out?"

Raymond drove in total silence. His anger filled the car like an odor. Marcia sat very still beside him and tried to will the speed of the car down in her head. She felt suddenly as if she were in a falling elevator, the cable snapped, somewhere in an old nightmare. The thought that she was going to die, that they would hit a patch of ice made her open her eyes. "Let me *out!*" she screamed.

Mysteriously the huge car slowed to a perfect, soundless

halt. Raymond reached across her and opened her door. He did not watch her get out but screeched the tires on the gravel before she had a chance to shut the door.

Marcia touched her blowing hair. Her forehead was damp and had already begun to freeze. She picked off a tiny piece of ice and looked at it under a streetlight, just before it melted away.

Marcia knew Mother would wait up for her so she opened the kitchen door and then the refrigerator door conspicuously, as if nothing had happened.

"Marcia?"

"It's me."

Mother trundled downstairs in her bathrobe. "I was worried about you," she said. "Where were you?"

"Oh, no place. We were just driving around talking. The ocean was pretty tonight." Marcia poured herself a large glass of milk. She gulped it down, but the coldness against her teeth made her wince and gasp.

"You look a fright! Are you sure you're all right?"

"Sure. I just drank too fast."

"You're very late. You know that, Marcia. You promised to be in by ten-thirty."

"I'm sorry. We just forgot the time. The clock in Raymond's car wasn't working."

Mother started washing out the glass. It was evident to Marcia that she was forming sentences about something she didn't want to discuss. Marcia tried to ease her way upstairs.

"Marcia, I want to talk to you a minute."

"Look, nothing happened. I just . . . we just didn't look at the time."

"Your face is beet red. You look as if you've been out in the cold for hours. What have you been doing?"

"I . . . well, I walked a little."

Mother leaned back tentatively against the stove, folding and then unfolding her arms. "Please, Marcia," she said, "I don't want you to think I was never young like you—that all I do is scold you. I just want you to be able to talk to me."

"Okay. I got out of the car and walked home. That's why I'm late."

"Why? What happened?"

"He was driving too fast. You told me I should always get out of the car and walk if someone drives too fast, and I did." Marcia could not make out Mother's face in the half-light of the kitchen, but she did see Mother's hand reach out as if to touch her lightly on the hair. Marcia drew back, and so immediately did the hand.

"Well, that's nice to know. I'm so glad you did that. You must be freezing. Would you like some cocoa?"

"No thanks. Well, okay." That was the right answer, she sensed. If Mother had anything horrible hidden in her thoughts waiting to be said, it would be better to appear cooperative.

Mother turned happily to the cabinet and began to assemble cups and saucers. Marcia had guessed right. She took the chance of sitting down at the kitchen table.

"You know, I don't know if I ever mentioned this, but when I was little, my mother used to make cocoa for us when we came in from sledding. I can still see her to this day and that funny old box of Droste's with the little Dutch children on it . . . " Mother's voice drifted off. "I guess I was a little younger than you," she added.

"That's nice," said Marcia.

"When I was your age I went out with boys too. We had a wonderful time."

Marcia looked at Mother neutrally. She thought of her

father's nervousness on trips to the hospital in New Bedford and on the way to pick up Sharon that time. She didn't know Mother was capable of this cheerful edginess. She must remember to say the right thing.

"I remember my first date. His name was Michael . . . Michael something. It was the funniest thing." Mother laughed as merrily as if this had been a party. "You know, I think I'll even whip some cream. Cocoa's no good without whipped cream. We'll forget about the calories for tonight."

Marcia was not thinking about calories.

"As I was saying. It was the funniest thing. We got a flat tire on the way home from a fraternity party. They had fraternities in high school then, and you know something? That boy had never changed a flat in his life. *I* had to change it, and when I got in the door, an hour late and covered with grease, I thought my father would die! I wasn't allowed to go out for a month. The dress belonged to my sister's best friend and I had to pay twenty dollars for it. Twenty dollars was a lot of money in those days."

"Gee" was all Marcia could think to say.

Mother measured out two tablespoons of cocoa, leveling off the top of the spoon as she always did. "We didn't have a lot of money, but we did have a lot of fun," she said.

"I guess you must have."

"That was many years ago. Things have certainly changed."

"I guess they have."

"You didn't know Mr. Van Dam very well. He was a wonderful man."

"Yes . . . I know."

"You know something, Marcia? In my day there were just as many girls who . . . ran around . . . who weren't virgins as there are today. Nothing has really changed."

"I guess it hasn't."

"I'll never forget when Mr. Van Dam was taking me out. I'd been seeing him for three or four months. He took me home one night and he asked me, 'May I kiss you?' I'll never forget that night. I decided I would marry him right then and there. Of course I didn't say so." The electric beater buzzed through the whipped cream. "It was just as important to him that we wait until after we were married as it was for me. Believe me, it wasn't easy for either of us. He didn't want to marry me until he graduated and got a job so he could support me. That took two and a half years. Then I had to graduate too and I was a year and a half behind him. But it was worth it."

"I guess so," said Marcia.

"That evening is one of my most treasured memories."

Marcia stared at a trivet that had been hung on the wall under the cuckoo clock. In fanciful iron letters it said:

> *God grant me the strength to change*
> *what I cannot accept,*
> *The serenity to accept what I*
> *cannot change,*
> *And the wisdom to know the difference.*

She thought about the words for a moment and decided they were hiding something in their perfect logic.

"Marcia, I don't want this to be a lecture. If you'll just hear me out?"

"Okay. Yes, I'm listening." Marcia brought Mother's face into focus again.

"Everybody wants to have fun. But the decisions you make now will affect you all your life. I know it's hard to picture, but someday you'll be my age. You will want to look back with pride on what you've done—both for yourself and the man you eventually marry. If you don't love that man, it'll be no good at all. If you waste everything now, you'll be jaded. Do you know what *jaded* means?"

"Yes." Marcia guessed around the general meaning of the word.

"That's what's happening to everyone around you. Young people seem to have no respect for their own lives later on, not to mention for their elders. Everything isn't for today. If you save yourself for the man you really love, your chances of happiness will be greatly increased. If you experience all these things now, pill or no pill—and I'm not going to pry and ask you what you do with Raymond—but you'll never be happy if—"

"Why not?" Marcia had not meant to ask that question.

"Because sex doesn't last forever. Even if you're married it dies down after a while, at least in women it does. Then you have to depend on your love for one another . . . that's *so* much better and more important than sex. It isn't easy."

"It doesn't sound easy," said Marcia.

"Do you think Raymond is that kind of a boy?"

"What kind of a boy?"

"Someone you could feel that way about . . . someone you want to marry? I don't think he is, Marcia. Forgive me, but I can see things you can't . . . don't yet have the—"

"Mother, I'm not going to *marry* him, for God's sake." Marcia watched carefully as Mother let the "for God's sake" go.

"Raymond is a fine-looking boy. I'm sure he is a very nice person. I know his father works hard . . . his mother works too . . . Marcia, this is very hard to say without sounding as if I were . . . well, a snob." Mother stopped and collected herself after the word *snob*. "But Raymond . . . that type of person is not for you. You've come so far. You've changed so much. Look at your schoolwork. You don't hear it yourself, I'm sure, but you speak completely differently from when you first came into our family. Raymond is the sort of person who . . . litters."

"Who what?"

"Who *litters* is what I said. He's from a family that keeps a broken icebox and I don't know what-all right out on their front lawn. He's the kind of person who throws cigarette packs out car windows. He looks like a *hood* in that motorcycle jacket. He chews gum. He stands with his hands in his pockets and doesn't even say hello. When he calls on the telephone he never says, 'Is Marcia there, *please*.' He has no manners."

"He doesn't mean to . . . he's just shy, that's all."

"Marcia, do you think I'm an old fogy? I'm not going to prevent you from going out with him. I just wish you'd see some other boys too."

"Well, they have to ask, you know."

"Will you?"

"They have to ask me first, Mother."

"Then you will."

"Okay."

"Do you think I'm an old fogy?"

"No," said Marcia with a sigh. "I think you're probably trying to help me the best you can, that's all."

She had said the right thing. Mother collected the two empty cocoa cups and got up looking very pleased.

Words, Marcia thought as she walked slowly from the kitchen. Why do they always mean two things at once? Why do I always dream—most of the time—when people talk to me?

Marcia did not expect to see Raymond in front of school where he always waited for her, but Monday morning he was there as usual.

"Get home all right Saturday night?" he asked.

"Yeah, sure. I was a little cold though."

"I came back for you. I looked for you. You must have taken another way home."

"I did. I walked by the sea the whole way."

"That must have been even colder."

"I don't think it made that much difference."

"Hey?"

"Yes."

"I'm sorry, Kim. I'm sorry I said all those things."

"Oh, Raymie, you—"

"Can I carry your books?"

Marcia allowed him to carry her books to her locker. "I really got it from the old man when I got home," he said, looking much cheered. "The car we had. The customer noticed the mileage last time he brought it in to have it fixed. He writes it down. I spent five hours turning back his odometer in the freezing cold, goddam him!"

It occurred to Marcia that she should have been angry with Raymond, but the moment was lost. Somewhere, far inside, there must be a lump of anger, she thought. She looked up for a moment at Raymond's long, angular body. He slouched against her open locker door, one hand running nervously through his hair, the other jingling change in his pocket. She wanted to say, "Please don't do that!" Jingling change was a habit she didn't like. She tried to feel angry as she stacked her books in her locker and took out others. The wires are disconnected, she told herself feebly. No current—only a deep smooth pool inside. Everything at the bottom of that pool is going to stay there. I can grope, but I can't come up with anything, good or bad.

The bell rang. Marcia rushed to her homeroom. She had five minutes and a study hall to finish her chemistry homework. If she did not finish it, she would have to face Sue Sturgiss and

None of the Above

Penny Loomis without it. She did not know quite what they would do, but she didn't want to take any chances. Most days they simply copied her answers and some of the work from her problems and passed them in. When there was a test in class they included her in their cheating circle. Penny did the adding and subtracting. Sue, who was a little better in math, did the multiplying and dividing, and Marcia, who was always prepared anyway, did the chemistry part of the questions. Marcia was thrilled to be included in this group. The gossip column in the school paper, called "The Tattler," had already referred to it obliquely. Sue's best friend, Val, who wrote for the school paper, put down "Who are those resourceful three who have a team in chemistree?" in the last issue of the paper. Marcia was a member of the secret three. She had never been mentioned in the school paper before. She still felt as if she were in the presence of famous people when she giggled and passed notes back and forth to Penny and Sue. She waited giddily for their approval, their laughter at her jokes. As long as she did their homework, she got it.

"Poor Miss Olson," as everyone called her, smiled benignly as Marcia's class strolled in. She wasn't fussy about people being late. She was attractive in a blowsy sort of a way, and during the last period of the day her boyfriend would drive up near the window in a blue Porsche and hand her a popsicle. This always made Miss Olson blush, but she always took the popsicle anyway, with apologies to the class. She was an easy teacher. If you came in for help just one time after class she wouldn't fail you.

"It seems to me," said Miss Olson hesitantly, "that a certain three people are getting identical answers in their homework. You know who you are and I assume you will discontinue this in the future."

Mercifully, no one turned around to look, but later in class

Marcia felt the sudden hardness of Penny's manner and the disinterest of Sue Sturgiss. She wanted to cry out to them, "Look, it's not my fault! You took the answers from *me*. I did the work!" But she could only look down in a red hot shame that the others didn't seem to feel at all. She wanted to apologize to Miss Olson after class but thought better of it when she saw the two girls watching her very closely.

Sue and Penny greeted Marcia enthusiastically as she and Raymond joined the group for Cokes at the drugstore after school.

"It seems to me," Penny Loomis mimicked Miss Olson.

"It seems to me," Sue took it up, laughing. "It seems to me some people are getting identical answers . . ." Her voice rose to a whiny pitch but she had to stop because her imitation made her laugh so hard.

"That nut who drives up in the Porsche," Penny said, pushing her golden hair over her shoulders. "What he sees in her I'd like to know."

"And those popsicles," said Sue. "Somebody ought to report her to Mr. Browning for that."

Marcia felt their cruelty in the pit of her stomach. She tried to laugh with them, but she liked Miss Olson and she liked the boyfriend with the popsicles.

"Well, we'll just have to change a few answers next time," said Penny. "She can't prove anything."

Penny Loomis had violet eyes. She went steady with Jimmy Goslau, who was the quarterback on the football team. Penny had announced her intention of following Jimmy to Tulane, where she would be a cheerleader just as she was now. She would be on national television, she said, because some of Tulane's games were televised. Marcia's father watched these games in the fall. He always had something nice to say about the cheerleaders. The announcers on television also watched the cheerleaders, and when the cameras lingered on them, they said things like "Just a little bird-doggin'!"

One wild fall afternoon, when Jimmy had made the winning pass in a football game, Marcia had seen him sweep Penny into his arms right in the middle of "Give me a G!" as he came off the field, and the crowd came tumbling down from the grandstand. He french-kissed her right there in front of everyone. Penny had looked a little surprised at first, but then she perched herself triumphantly on Jimmy's shoulder and waved to the crowd like a celebrity. Marcia had looked up enviously at Penny's long, smooth legs, but she was shocked by the frightening hardness of those violet eyes, and she had turned to Raymond, who did not play football because of his asthma, and squeezed his hand. Raymond put his hand on her hair and then her shoulders and led her off the field. He told everyone he couldn't play football because of a trick knee.

"Party at Woody's house Friday," said Sue. She pulled one of Woody's sideburns affectionately.

"I don't know if I can," said Marcia.

"What do you mean? It's Friday, isn't it?"

"I know, but we're having an English test Monday, and Mother might . . ."

"You tell her if we're having a test?"

"No, but Chrissy will. Her class is having one too, and she won't even study for it but she'll hear about it and tell Mother sure as anything. She always does."

"Boy!" Sue sucked in her breath and stared wide-eyed at Marcia. "Chris Van Dam, what a . . . what did your old man marry her mother for anyhow, Kim? He doesn't seem so bad."

Everyone at the table appeared to be interested in this question. Marcia flung out her hands hopelessly at their anticipation. "I don't know," she said, looking at Raymond as if he might provide her with an answer. "He was very lonely,

I guess. He needed a wife. He knew my sister was going to get married. He was married to my mother for twenty years or something. I don't know. Maybe you sort of get used to being married . . . they get along now, better. I guess she was lonely too. She needed a man around. Same thing, sort of. They had a nice honeymoon." Marcia had said more than she wanted to.

"Well, why don't you ask your father if you can go to parties instead?" Sue asked with an odd note of what must have been respect for the dead in her voice.

"I'll probably be able to go. I'll study Saturday," said Marcia.

"Such a brain!" said Sue, but Raymond gave her an awful look and said, "Where would you be without her, I'd like to know? Failing chemistry!"

"Who cares?"

"You want to stay back? You want to stay in this dump an extra year?"

"Raymie, you're cute when you're angry!"

Marcia started collecting her books. Raymond stood up and took them from her. I could never say anything like that, she told herself. You're so cute when you're mad!—I wouldn't even *think* of it. Maybe I'll try it next time. But she knew she wouldn't have the courage. It was so hard for her to be like them. Next time . . . always next time she would do this or say that the way Penny had or Sue had, but next time never seemed to come or if it did she found herself swallowing her words. Rather than saying the wrong thing, she said nothing. Some tension had established itself at the table that both frightened and pleased Marcia. The others had seen just a glimmering of the anger in Raymond that frightened her so, but since it was in her behalf it was a little exciting.

Raymond wore the mysteries of his first two years in another high school around himself like a shroud. Not many people could have done what he did—break into the popular crowd in the middle of junior year. Perhaps it was because he was good looking or came from the city and acted in surly, confident city ways with the other boys. He took her hand as they left the drugstore and gave her a private smile that aroused her when she saw that Penny and Sue had taken note of it.

"So you think you can come, don't you?" he asked. Marcia smiled. She felt he must want her or he wouldn't ask. She began preparing herself for a long Saturday night with *Hamlet*. How anyone, how Chrissy could read things like that in the original and answer questions in class without having once looked at the questions in the Monarch Notes version, she did not know.

"How come you never talk about what you did before you came to Gloucester?" Marcia asked. They were walking to Woody's party. Raymond could not get a car for the night.

"What do you mean?" Marcia knew he would say that.

"Well, about where you lived, for instance."

"I told you. Mattapan—outside Boston. Then when my uncle died, my old man came up here to run his garage. He still supports my uncle's wife and kids."

"Your aunt."

"Yeah. I never see her."

"What was it like in Mattapan?"

"Oh, you know, same thing pretty much. There were junkies though. I had to go to Catholic school. I mean my old man said I had to because of all the junkies and stuff in the public school. The nuns were a whole lot nastier than the teachers here. Every place is pretty much the same though."

Marcia didn't want to keep on asking questions. Raymond did not ask many questions himself; he didn't seem to like them. "I still miss New Bedford sometimes," she said.

"Yeah?"

"I liked it better there, I think."

"How come? I've been to New Bedford. It's a crummy town compared to this."

"Oh, I don't know. Maybe because Mamma was alive and all. I really don't still miss her though. Maybe it was the kids. My friends. I never made friends again like I had there."

"What do you mean? You have plenty of friends."

"Not really."

"What about Penny and Sue and Val and the kids?"

"Oh, they're all right. But I get the feeling they don't like me that much. Mostly they're your friends, Raymie."

Raymond whistled through his teeth at this. "You worry too much," he said.

"Yes, but I don't have . . . well, like a best friend anymore. I used to see a lot of Carol, but well, she's just not in that crowd and this year I'm in three pilot classes and I just don't get to see her."

Raymond walked with his hands jammed deep in his blue-jeans pockets. He never wore gloves. "Carol Kubiak," he said. "She's a creep. She thinks her freckles are so cute, and the way she walks. No wonder no guy'll look at her!"

Marcia realized with a little start that she and Carol had both tried to imitate the way Penny Loomis walked. Carol must have kept it up in school. Marcia would never have dared to imitate Penny outside of her own bedroom with only Carol to watch and laugh. "Don't be mean, Raymie," she said.

"I'm not being mean . . . well, the truth hurts. What do you need her for? You've got me."

"Oh, Raymie. I just said that I didn't have any good friends in that group. That's all. None of those kids even knew who I was before I started going with you. I mean, you could go out with Penny or Sue or any one of them. But I'm not pretty and, well, you know . . . popular like them, like you, you know, *accepted*."

"Bullshit!"

"Raymie, how come you do go out with me? You could—"

"You ask too many questions."

"But I want to know!"

Raymond bent down and made a large snowball with his bare hands. Marcia started to run.

"Don't you dare throw that at me!" she shrieked. "No fair!" But he caught hold of her coat and pretended he was going to squash it down her neck. "I'm sorry," she said, laughing now because she could see he wasn't really angry.

"Father, bless me," said Raymond, holding the snowball out of reach above her head. Marcia backed up and leaned against a tree.

"Father bless me," she yelled, panting, "for I have sinned."

"What have you done, my child?" Raymond asked, his voice mocking a flat Boston Irish tenor.

"I ask too many questions, Father," Marcia repeated, "and I put myself down again."

"Those are mortal sins, my child," said Raymond. "Ten Hail Marys and a Lord's Prayer."

"Hail Mary, full of grace. The Lord is with thee. Blessed art thou among women and blessed is the fruit of thy womb, Jesus. Hail Mary, full of—"

"You forgot the rest of it, the second part," coached Raymond, almost seriously, with the snowball still in his hand.

"I'm . . . out of breath, Raymie. Please don't make me. I can never remember it anyway."

"Well, okay," said Raymond. "Ego te absolvo, in nomine Patris et Filii et Spiritus Sancti. Amen." He dropped the snowball and put his arm warmly around her. Raymond had taught her parts of Confession and Our Father the Catholic way.

Every once in a while he would make her say them, for what reason Marcia did not know. Raymond seemed to think it was hilarious, however, and he doubled up with laughter at the mistakes she made. Marcia did not consider it wise to laugh at anyone's religion, but since Raymond was Catholic and she was not, perhaps it was all right.

Penny Loomis acknowledged Marcia with a heft of her beer can. She sat on Jimmy Goslau's lap, Jimmy's long arms wrapped around her and strumming chords at random on his guitar. Marcia reminded herself to compliment him on the guitar. She had been told that it was new, Spanish, and had cost over four hundred dollars. Another girl, someone's visiting cousin, Amanda, tootled away on a recorder in the corner.

Marcia sat down cross-legged on the floor, next to the record player, and made herself look busy eating handfuls of potato chips. She watched wistfully as Raymond made the rounds of his friends, coming up behind them with a put-on karate chop and a short, masculine laugh. He stripped off his leather jacket and flung it toward a chair, but it slipped to the floor and stood up on its end as if it still contained him. She wondered idly whether he even owned an overcoat, if he had a closet somewhere in a bedroom of his own . . . how he would be with his parents at dinner in the evenings. It embarrassed Raymond to talk about his home and family. He seemed to want to pretend that they didn't exist at all or that he himself didn't exist in the hours he was not with her or his friends. Raymond lit a cigarette and let it dangle from his fingers. He only lit cigarettes most of the time. Occasionally he brought them up to his mouth like the other boys. He had had asthma as a child . . . a child in a town called Mattapan. Marcia mouthed the word *Mattapan* to herself. How like a children's sandbox game it sounded. It made Raymond seem smaller as she said it again. She realized that there must have been a time when he had not owned a Harley-Davidson. She watched him open a second can of beer with a snap and toss the metal ring into a nearby plant. She edged closer to Amanda with the recorder.

"That's a hard-looking thing to play," she said.

Amanda looked curiously at Marcia for a moment. She played a quick scale and said, "Not really."

"Can I see it?"

"Sure."

Marcia wiped the mouthpiece on her sleeve. The girl made a face that said she didn't like that. "Here," she said impatiently. "Hold your thumb over this hole. That's E like a clarinet. Then . . . let me show you." Amanda took back the recorder and blew several notes, naming them each time. Marcia nodded gravely and made it a point not to wipe off the mouthpiece again. Amanda watched Marcia position her fingers. Then she lost interest and joined some people in the kitchen.

Marcia tried to imitate exactly what Amanda had done. She blew several notes quietly to herself, and although she couldn't remember their names, her fingers were placed correctly and the sounds were dramatic, reminiscent of some pungent August evening in a movie she had seen years ago. After a time Marcia was able to make two notes unwaveringly, then four, then six. She was so pleased with herself that she thought of borrowing the recorder and learning to play in earnest, but Mother's reaction would be one of such delight— she would say Marcia should join the school orchestra, that playing a musical instrument would impress college acceptance boards—that Marcia decided against it. A shame, she reflected. For the moment she let the solemn notes absorb her, burying her worries under a blanket of woody melancholy.

"Hey, Raymie! Will you tell that stupid girl of yours to cut it out! I can't concentrate on my chords." Jimmy Goslau's angry voice rang out across the room to Marcia like a spontaneous fissure in the floor. She saw several people turn to look at her. Penny was still sitting in Jimmy's lap. The cheerful violet eyes caught Marcia's eyes for an instant and Penny snickered. Then she went back to caressing Jimmy's hair. Marcia dropped the recorder and snatched up her coat and was out the door before she could even get her arms through the sleeves. She had almost reached the end of the street when Raymond caught up with her.

"Wait!" he shouted. "Jesus, don't cry, don't cry, he didn't mean it."

Marcia hurried along without looking at him. She was *not* crying. The tears came from the stinging wind in her face. Raymond ran backward, trying to get her attention.

"Look, I'm sorry that happened, Kim. I'm sorry. I punched him out!"

"You punched him *out!*" Marcia wiped her nose on the sleeve of her coat without thinking.

"No, I didn't exactly punch him out. But I did give him a good shake. I knocked that whore and that frigging guitar off his lap. The bastard—I could have broken his head!"

"What do you care anyway?" Marcia asked. "Those kids think I'm stupid. What do you care?"

"Please, let's go back," said Raymond, shivering. He had never said please before, that she could recall. He had forgotten his jacket. Marcia wanted to laugh cruelly at the Superman S on his T-shirt but she turned around and kept walking.

"No, I'm not going back there—ever," she said.

"Well, I'll walk you home then."

"You don't have to. I can find my own way."

"I will anyway. I don't want to go back there either."

Marcia walked on sullenly. "Do what you like," she said with a shrug. Raymond followed her at a distance of two or three steps past the blocks of darkened houses. Someone's dog barked angrily at them from a garage. Marcia could see out of the corner of her eye that he was still there, still shivering.

"For God's sake, you're going to catch pneumonia," she said impatiently, coming to a stop.

"I could go back for my jacket . . . if you'd wait?"

"It's too cold to wait."

"Well, I'll keep going then."

After a while she unbuttoned her coat and gave him half over his shoulders. Raymond had to walk with his legs bent to keep it on, but he managed and they both laughed.

"Nobody home?"

"They're all at the movies. Some foreign flick. That's how come I got to go tonight, partly, because Chris wanted to go with them." Marcia thought briefly of *Quatre Cents Coups* and of Jerry with the red hair (for she had forgotten that it was a little boy in the movie) running along the beach, coming closer to her.

"Your old man have any brandy or anything? It's about a hundred below out there."

"Nothing. They never drink in this house. I can make us some coffee though."

Marcia felt formal, a little like Mother as she stood at the stove with the coffee pot. Raymond looked around at the kitchen. He had been in the kitchen many times before, but now that it was empty of her family he seemed to want to study it. He noticed the trivet and chuckled.

"She likes things like that," Marcia explained.

"My old lady puts up stuff too," said Raymond. "Different though. She has this big picture of Jesus. You look one way at it and the eyes are closed. You look the other way and the eyes are open and his heart is gushing blood. This isn't all that different though. It's all junk." He glanced again at the trivet. "Reminds me of a novena," he said with a smile.

"What's that?"

"I bet they don't go to church."

"Well, only sometimes. Christmas and Easter and Palm Sunday. Daddy hates it. He falls asleep and Mother gets embarrassed. What's a novena?"

"A prayer. A prayer to a specific saint."

"But you don't go to church either," said Marcia, not knowing whether he was being critical or not.

"I know," he said. "I don't anymore. Not since Immaculate Heart . . . that's where I went before. But you never forget that stuff. I used to have nightmares. This sister. I had her in third grade. She . . . maybe it was fourth grade." Raymond looked up. "Ah, the hell with it."

"What, Raymie?"

"Oh, she thought I did something I never did. I know the son of a bitch who did it. But I never told. She whaled the shit out of me one day. Told my old lady. My old lady put me in a closet until my old man got home. He took off his belt and beat the shit out of me too. Sister Angelica was her name."

"But didn't you tell them you hadn't done it? What did they think you did, anyway?"

"Oh, nothing. Just stupid kid stuff. It wasn't anything."

"It couldn't have been nothing if your mother put you in—"

"Well, okay. This kid, his name was Mickey Daly. He was backwards, you know, crazy. All the bigger kids were always beating up on him, and so I never told, but his old man had a butcher shop, and Mickey used to bring in stuff, you know. Well, one day he put a pig's heart in the Sister's drawer and got somebody, probably his brother, to write her a note saying Jesus' heart was right there in her desk. Well, the Sister opened the drawer and when she saw it she just . . . they had to carry her out. Later she let me have it because I was laughing. I was the only one who laughed, I guess."

"Raymie, that's just awful . . . about your mother putting you in a closet and all. If anybody did that to me, I'd just die."

"You're a girl," said Raymond shrugging. "Even my old lady wouldn't do that to a girl, I don't think. Let's see what's on the late movie."

Marcia could hear him in the living room switching channels back and forth. She washed the coffee pot carefully, delaying as long as she could the moment when she would have to go in and curl up next to him on the sofa—Mother's chintz-covered colonial sofa that Sharon and Moose had once . . .

"I guess I should thank you," she said as he began to ease himself down on top of her.

"For what?"

"Oh, I don't know. Rescuing me from awful Jimmy Goslau, maybe?"

"You don't have to thank me," said Raymond, and he snapped off the light above her head.

Raymond's hands didn't move over her as roughly as they usually did, Marcia noticed, nor did he grip her with such ferocity that she thought her arms would break like matchsticks. He didn't go into his frenzied, hurtful motion that took her breath away. She waited, tentatively. It almost seemed as if he wanted to go to sleep. No one else was in the house, Marcia remarked to herself. For the first time there was no chance of someone upstairs coming by and knocking teasingly on the door, then running away with a great clatter, laughing. No one was downstairs to see them, to make jokes afterward.

She relaxed slowly and listened to the words he spoke in her hair, most of them drowned out by the cars passing in the slush outside. She warned herself lazily that she ought to be careful now. Something was starting up, something could happen, but the warning voice and then another voice—which she realized was her own, out loud—seemed to come from another room and then from so far away that they didn't matter at all. "Oh, please, I want you to . . ." she heard herself say, and she was shocked by her own words. She felt Raymond's fingers cautiously moving up the inside of her leg, where he had never touched her before. She could not stop herself from taking his hand, unzipping her slacks in front, and putting it inside where the swollen, unrelenting part of her compelled her to put it. Nothing mattered except that Raymond must not get up or tell her to stop what she was doing until the livid point, just ahead of her, was over.

When Marcia opened her eyes, she found him gazing quite dejectedly at her. She expected his silent fury right away. She knew she had done something terribly wrong and stupid. Maybe he would hit her. Boys did that. Maybe all those things Mother had said about people with refrigerators in their front yards were true. What have I done? she asked herself. I lost control for just a minute. Please, God. I'll never do it again.

"Raymie, are you mad at me?" she made herself ask aloud. He didn't answer.

"Oh, Raymie, I'm sorry. I guess I did something awful. I don't know what happened."

"Stop it! Stop apologizing," he said.

"But . . . I'm afraid you're going to be mad . . . you are mad. I . . . it was awful. I'll never . . ."

"There's nothing to apologize *for*." He moved over to the coffee table, where he had left his cigarettes, on his hands and knees. Then he sat opposite her on the floor. "Was it awful?" he asked. "How the hell do you think that makes me feel?"

"What?"

"It wasn't awful. Why should it be? There's nothing wrong with you."

"But . . ."

"For Chrissakes at least don't say it was awful."

"Okay," said Marcia meekly.

"Was it nice?"

"Yes."

"Okay," he said and stared at the cigarette he had taken out as if it were a charm. Then he threw it down.

"Raymie, I don't understand."

"Okay," he said. He was trembling all over, vibrating like Chrissy's tuning fork, Marcia thought. "It's . . . me," he said. "I'm . . . it's my . . . fault. I can't."

"You . . . can't what?"

"Look . . . I'm not . . . I'm not a real man, I . . ." but he couldn't explain. He looked up at her as if she could say it for him. Marcia tried to believe that she hadn't been stupid and that he was not angry at her.

"Everything," he said, hiding his eyes behind his hand. "I'm a phony, if you want to know. You wouldn't believe it. I thought everything would be different here . . . that I could make it different. I thought I . . . before, where I came from, I couldn't make it with any girl. Some one of them, Louise McKay, McKenna, that was her name. How could I forget? She told everybody. Somehow it got out. Somebody left . . . some creep left girl's . . . girl's . . . a piece of girl's . . . underwear in my locker. I knew who it was. I tried to strangle him with it. I had him down on the floor of the boys' locker room. He was smaller than me. He kept saying, 'Don't rape me, Raymond!' The harder I hit him, the more he laughed. Somebody pulled me off. She told. The little whore. They all . . . they all stood around laughing. All of them, naked. Telling me I was a . . . a . . .

"I thought it would be different here. When my uncle died I was so happy. I thought I could get into the fast crowd. No one would know. *What a phony.* Even the Harley. The Hell's Angels. I worked all summer in a soft drink factory in Revere to get that Harley. I was so scared on that damn thing at first, you wouldn't believe. But I made myself. I see all those guys out there on Route 1 by the MacDonald's and I want to kill them. I don't know why. But this thing, with girls . . . I started going with Betty Thompson but I knew it was going to happen again. I couldn't put anything over on her be-cause . . . I couldn't take a chance. She was too smart. She'd been going with Woody for two years and they . . . he . . . Christ! So I started going with you because . . . because . . ."

Marcia's thoughts whispered to her, Because I'm such a nothing, so stupid I wouldn't know. "Because maybe you thought I wouldn't tell anyone, like Louise McKenna did. Raymie?" she asked.

"Yes," he said. She could barely hear him.

"I won't. Of course I won't."

"But you'll never want to see me again."

"What?"

"There's a word for . . . what I am. I know very well what it is. I can't say it . . ."

Marcia had never seen a man cry. She supposed they did when wars came or when their wives or children died, but her father had not cried at her mother's death, and now here was this great lump of a boy, almost a man, sobbing like an infant in her lap.

"It'll get better, Raymie. I know it will. I promise it will."

He said nothing.

"We'll work it out, you'll see," she said, looking question-ingly at the cowlick in his hair. "And I won't leave," she added.

"Jesus," said Raymond. "I love you."

Marcia knew only that she had said the right thing.

Seventeen

"Now I know what Carla's going to say the minute she gets here."

Marcia nibbled on a Christmas cookie. "What's Carla going to say?" she asked.

"She's going to try and persuade you to go to that dreadful place in New York where she went."

"You mean Sarah Lawrence, Mother."

"Yes. I talked with her on the phone the other night, and when she heard Chrissy was accepted at Yale, that's the first thing she said. Carla's a nice girl, Marcia, but she isn't . . . she isn't your type. I have nothing against the Jewish people, and God knows even your father thinks State of Israel Bonds are a good investment, but Sarah Lawrence is full, *full* of nothing but a certain type of city Jew. You wouldn't have any friends, anything in common . . ." Mother looked up from the holly she was wiring into a wreath. "Are you listening, Marcia?"

"Of course."

"Who is Mr. Sisson? Is he your guidance counselor or is he the head of the department?"

"He's both."

"Well, I checked with him last week, and he said if you pull up your history grade this term and particularly that C in English, you won't have a thing to worry about as far as U. Mass. is concerned."

"I know."

"He was very pleased with the improvement in your college boards, by the way."

Marcia sighed. She continued roping gold tinsel around three cardboard angels that were to be placed on the mantelpiece. Mother had made the angels herself. She had made the dark brown pine-cone wreath on the door, and the windows were strung with popcorn and walnuts and ornaments of Mother's own design. Marcia enjoyed helping prepare for Christmas. Chrissy was off somewhere. Chrissy said she hated Christmas and privately, to Marcia, she had said that this would be her very last one at home. Mother needed someone to enjoy the decorating with. Besides, Marcia had always liked the colored lights and evergreens and boxes of cookies Mother turned out at this time of year.

"I bet you're excited about seeing your nephew for the first time!"

Marcia hesitated. Then she remembered her nephew was Sharon and Buddy's baby, Anthony Jr. "Yes, she sure writes a lot about him. I mean, when she writes." Since Marcia had last seen her sister, the fact of Sharon's predicament at that time had evaporated as far as everyone was concerned.

"Well, she probably doesn't have much time to write," Mother said, tightening the wire around yet another pine-cone wreath, "with the baby and all, and maybe she's afraid of boring you with the details. It's been two years since she's seen you. You've changed a great deal. Sharon probably has too."

Marcia nodded in fuzzy agreement. She was thinking about the books Carla had given her. Carla had brought her *The Vicar of Wakefield* and *Look Homeward Angel* on her last visit. She wanted to tell Carla, yes, she'd read them, yes she'd enjoyed them very much. Carla would not question her about them, but she would be delighted that Marcia had read them. It was curious how reading a book could gratify Carla as much as an expensive gift. Carla would also take it as a good sign that Marcia now wore blue jeans and an army jacket. Chrissy, of course, did too, but for Mother's sake Marcia kept her clothing neat and clean.

"This is where we always had the tree when Mr. Van Dam was alive," said Mother. "I know your father thinks it looks better in the middle of the room, but I think it's nicer here."

"It looks fine either way to me," said Marcia.

"I'm sure it does . . . I guess it doesn't matter really, but some things . . . I don't know what it is, but Christmas makes me think of him. You must have certain things that make you think of your mother too."

Marcia tried to remember Christmas with her mother, but all she could conjure up was a kindly fat form in a duster, moving slowly as if underwater, watching TV . . . what was it? . . . "As the World Turns," of course.

"Don't break those scissors! They're my sewing scissors!"

"I'm sorry," said Marcia. "I didn't realize."

"Have you asked Raymond for Christmas dinner yet?"

"He can't. He has to work."

"On Christmas?"

"Somebody has to be at the garage. It's the only one open in town and they get a lot of towing jobs on holidays."

"Would you like me to ask John to bring one of his friends from Harvard?"

"Mother!"

"Now you sound as bad as Chrissy," said Mother. She snipped off the ends of a satin bow, sprayed gold paint on it, and fastened it to a package. Marcia did not want to discuss Raymond any further, but she could feel Mother's thoughts gathering on the horizon like the cavalry.

"Well, as I've said before, I wish you'd go out with some-body else. There's no sense in sticking like a leech to Raymond when you're going to be leaving him in September. You should have fun, by all means, and Raymond is a nice boy, but I'm afraid you might be getting too serious. You're just going to hurt him in the end. You should think of that."

"Please, Mother."

"I mean it. Has he asked you to marry him? What does he think he's going to do when you go off to college?"

"I haven't decided to go to college."

"You *what*? You've applied to three colleges and you haven't decided to *go*?"

"I meant which college."

"Oh, well. That's better. I hope, by the way, that you do pull up that C. How did you manage to get a C?"

"I don't know. English. I can't understand Shakespeare very well."

"If you'd gone with us to the Stratford festival last summer, you might not be having this trouble. I told you then, and—"

"Mother! You saw, what was it? . . . *The Twelve Nights of Windsor* or something and—"

"The *Merry Wives of Windsor*."

"All right, The *Merry Wives of Windsor* . . . and we have *King Lear*, so what good would it have done?"

"It would have given you background, Marcia. It would have

helped. It would have given you a feel, a familiarity with Shakespeare. What do you think it is frankly, Marcia, that makes Chrissy . . . that made Yale accept Chrissy on early admission? *Early admission* for a *girl,* remember."

"Mother, please! I'm not Chrissy. I know how smart Chrissy is. Do you have to throw her in my . . . "

"I'm not throwing her up to you. I never said you should apply to Yale. I asked you a simple question. I'm making a simple point. Chrissy is interested in Shakespeare. She respects it. She loves it. That's why she can understand *King Lear* and why she wanted to go to Stratford and wrote for those tickets herself."

"Well, I'm sorry. I'm not. I hate it."

"You *think* you hate it, Marcia, because it's new to you in a way. The idea of enjoying Shakespeare will come to you. Believe me. It's impossible to hate the greatest writer in the English language."

"Not for me, it isn't."

"All right, Marcia. Maybe you do. But how about that C? Is *King Lear* so difficult? Can I help you with it? When Chrissy's father was alive we used to read aloud all the time. Supposing we did that, all of us . . . read *King Lear* aloud?"

"Mother, it's over anyway. We're doing Romantic poets now."

"Well, that sounds easier. If you bring up that C to, say, a B plus, Mr. Sisson says you'll have nothing to worry about. He says your 620 in English is fine." When Marcia did not reply, Mother added, "Marcia, you sound so . . . I just want the best for you, you know that, don't you?"

"I'll pull up the C, Mother," said Marcia. She was dreadfully embarrassed. Marcia did not like to think much about college, although she had dutifully applied to the University of Massachusetts, Rollins College in Florida, which Chrissy had said taught nothing but underwater basketweaving, and Sarah Lawrence, at Carla's insistence. Her teachers assured her she would be able to go anyplace within reason if she kept her marks up. She didn't know what "within reason" meant and didn't ask. She suspected that the admission boards would see right through her marks and her college board scores to that place in the center of her that still cared so little for books and words; that made her do her homework for the same reason she made her bed every morning and did the dishes at night— to avoid being told to do it and to silence the goading comparisons to Chrissy and her sister Sharon. She believed the letters of application she had so painstakingly typed would never be opened at all, that they would be blown as randomly as bits of grass in the wind to the dead-letter office.

"I think you'll be happy at U. Mass," said Mother. "The girls will be just right for you there."

Not too bright, not too dumb, just right for middling me, Marcia thought. She wondered how she had let that slip out about not going to college at all. She hadn't really known she'd been considering such a thing, except for a joking promise to Raymond the night before. Now that he was out of high school, he talked about buying a Buick franchise with his father in a couple of years and about finding a little house. The suggestion made Marcia uneasy. It was worse when he teased her about children. "I want a girl first," he insisted, although for some reason Marcia suspected this was not true.

Night fell quickly, before four o'clock in the afternoon. John and Carla arrived, and Chrissy came back from wherever she'd been, ecstatic at the sight of her brother. John swung her around in circles as he must have done when she'd been very little. "Stop it, Johnny! I'm getting dizzy!" she crowed, laughing, but Marcia could tell Chrissy could have gone on airplaning forever in her brother's arms.

"How's the old Yalie? How's the old Eli?" John asked sitting down and unbuttoning his coat. Then he broke into a falsetto version of the Whiffenpoof song.

"Better than creepy old Harvard!" said Chrissy happily. "Better than Crimson . . . what is it?"

"There's nothing wrong with Crimson Triumph," said John, pretending insult and he started to sing "With Crimson Triumph Flashing."

"Johnny, I'm so happy to see you!" said Chrissy and although she'd had nothing to do with it, she asked him didn't he think the house looked pretty.

Marcia was intrigued by Chrissy's exuberance, but she did feel a little shunted out by it, and by Christmas because she couldn't fervently share it with anyone. Perhaps with Raymond tomorrow night. But if there was any passion inside her, it had no electricity like Chrissy's. It lay deep in that pool, the inside pool. Her sister, the relatives, the baby would come tomorrow. Tonight, Christmas Eve, belonged to the family, and that meant Mother and Chrissy and John.

"Marcia did it all," Mother said. "Marcia helped me. She did the angels and the whole tree. I didn't do a thing! I think the tree looks lovely, just perfect!"

Marcia's father took the pipe from his mouth and admired the tree—yes, it looked better than it ever had before. And wasn't it an excellent tree? Mother went on. Marcia's father had chosen it down at the church, and it was so full and even they hadn't even had to cut off the top.

John and Carla put armfuls of packages on the white, spangled cloth under the Christmas tree. Mother reminded John how much she loved his crèche. He had carved it and painted it when he was nine and had added a new figure, an angel or a Wise Man every year until he'd gone away to Harvard. She said she wished he'd do one more when he had the time, someday when he was out of law school. Could he do a donkey? she wondered, because the old one had cracked apart altogether. "I've glued him every year," said Mother. "But this time his tail went and I couldn't find the leg. It must have been thrown out in last year's wrapping paper." John said Yes, he had a few days off before school started again. He would get some wood. It would be a good time to do it, while he was thinking about it.

"But Polk's is open till nine tonight," said Mother excitedly. She wanted to know if she ran up there and got the right kind of wood, could he do it right now? Do it for Christmas morning? She had his tools upstairs, surely they could be sharpened. Was there a whetstone in the garage? she wanted to know. Marcia's father said there probably was. John, with some resignation in his voice, said not to bother. He would go up to Polk's himself and pick out the wood. Chrissy announced she was going with him. Marcia noticed both a fierce kind of sorrow and happiness cross Mother's face in the space of a second as she warned them to go slowly, that it had been blowing outside since three o'clock and there was a coating of ice on the roads beneath the snow.

She thought Mother would actually break down and cry when the wood-carving tools could not be found. A search was made of all the closets and drawers, in among things that had been John's: hockey skates, a Boy Scout sash, and even an old wooden train that his grandfather had carved. Marcia wanted things to go smoothly, not to be disturbing. In vain she helped Mother look.

"What about a kitchen knife? Or a pen knife?" she suggested. But Mother turned on her angrily and said, "No, no, it must be done with the right tools. They were here somewhere." She knew no one had thrown them out.

John and Chrissy came back, however, with a piece of wood

and a brand-new knife, and Mother exuded such joy at John's resourcefulness that Marcia stepped back from her in amazement, as she might have done from a sizzling fire.

Everyone watched respectfully as John sat down at the dining-room table with a block of wood and some newspapers to catch the shavings. Dinner was served in the living room so as not to disturb him. Christmas carols, three albums of them, had been set on repeat on the record player. At one point Marcia noticed Mother holding her father's hand. She turned away, a little embarrassed, but pleased too because she knew Mother was trying to bring him into her Christmas. Just when things had settled down between them, she couldn't say. They hadn't even had a serious disagreement in a year, that she could remember. The picture of Mr. Van Dam had at last vanished from the bureau. I've grown accustomed too, she said to herself.

Marcia woke in the middle of the night with a sharp pain in her stomach. She tiptoed downstairs for a glass of milk. John was still working on the donkey. He had almost finished and it looked much more professional than the other figures in the crèche.

"How are you doing, Marsh?" he asked.

"Fine. Fine thank you," she said shyly.

He paused. Then he said, "Chris tells me you're seeing a lot of Raymond these days. She seems to think he's a really neat guy."

"She does? Chrissy said that?"

John allowed her words to hang in the air for a minute. Then he laughed softly. "No. Actually, now that you mention it, you're perfectly right, of course. Chrissy didn't say she liked him. There's no sense in my lying to you. But maybe because she didn't, I thought . . . Chrissy's just . . . well, when she gets a guy of her own, she'll probably think Raymond's another Jack Kennedy."

Marcia swallowed hard. "I wish . . ." she began, but she stopped. "Gee, that's a beautiful . . . that's a beautiful donkey you've made. I hope you leave it the way it is, without painting it. The wood is so pretty."

"No," said John, leaning back in his chair and rubbing his eyes. "I think she'd like it painted to match the others—to look like the old one that got broken."

Anthony Jr. wouldn't let Marcia or anyone but his mother come near him without screaming, and Sharon had to change his clothes at least five times on Christmas day. He arrived in a red-and-green Rudolph the Red-Nosed Reindeer suit, then he was changed to one with Santa Claus on the front. After that Sharon ran out of Christmas clothes. Marcia could not find much time to talk to her sister. Sharon, who had put on twenty pounds since her last pregnancy, was pregnant again, she announced, as she sat on the sofa next to Buddy. Buddy nodded in indifferent agreement. When Sharon asked Marcia about Raymond, Marcia found herself answering as coldly as she did to Mother. She wanted the old Sharon back, so that she could laugh with her and tell her everything, but this new Sharon talked only about layettes and teething and the people moving into the mobile home, twice as big as theirs, next door.

Carla got on quite well with Grandmother and Grand-father Van Dam, and Aunt Mim—just whose aunt she was, Marcia was not sure—but John walked around the house like a ghost, hating his name embroidered in white on a red Christmas stocking, grimacing at the Christmas carols that still played on repeat. Chrissy followed him from room to room as she always did when he was home. "Oh, Johnny, I wish you'd come home more. You never come anymore," Marcia over-heard Chrissy say.

"We came for Thanksgiving," he had answered hopelessly.

"I know, but you used to come for dinner all the time. Carla doesn't like it. Carla doesn't like us."

"Do you blame her that much?"

"What do you mean, 'Do I blame her?'"

"I wouldn't say she feels all that welcome here."

"Mom's nice to her. I'm nice to her. I like Carla. What do you mean?"

John chuckled at this. "You know who likes Carla?" he asked. "Marcia likes Carla. If Mother would stop dropping those dumb little hints about getting married all the time and if you weren't so jealous of your big brother, it might be easier for her."

"Boy, she suffers, doesn't she? She really suffers. She really has it tough."

"Chris."

"What," Chrissy had said, about to explode in tears.

"Just . . . just try to be a little nicer to Carla, okay? I mean I can't change Mom, but you . . . "

"What do you want me to do? Go up and throw my arms around her twenty times a day?"

John sighed. "For one thing," he began, "you don't have to prove how smart you are to her all the time. You're always dropping names . . ."

"Dropping *names!*" Chrissy dissolved in sobs.

John held her hand and sat down next to her. "Like Adler and Jung," he said kindly. "I know you read a lot and you know what you're talking about, but . . . "

"Okay, *okay*. Johnny, could you please tell Mom to stop trying to make me play Christmas carols on the damn piano. Please!"

"Please do it," John whispered. "Do it for her. It means so much to her."

"I'm pretty mad at you, by the way," Chrissy said, blowing her nose in his handkerchief. "You didn't say anything when she made that crack about my hair this morning. You're a great one for just sitting back and giving advice to other people. You don't even stick up for Carla when Mom says all that stuff about the Jews."

"She didn't knock the Jews."

"Hah. All about the Jews being such a *wonderful* people. What do you think she means by that?"

"That's not what's bothering you, is it?"

"What do you mean!"

"It's . . . well, it was that skirt this morning, wasn't it?"

Mother had made Chrissy a skirt and matching jacket for Christmas. Chrissy had had to model it for everyone. When she came downstairs in the skirt, she had it on backward. This had been pointed out by Mother in front of everyone. Chrissy turned flaming red and scuttled upstairs in tears. Marcia had ached for her.

Through most of Christmas day, Carla was coolly polite, but Marcia could see that Mother made things more difficult for her by mentioning Carla's "Jewish background."

"Well, it isn't as bad as last year," Marcia whispered sympathetically to her. "Just think, last year I got acne soap in my stocking. This year it was plain soap."

"It wouldn't be so bad if it were Yves Saint Laurent, but it was Camay," said Carla, flipping through the pages of *Time* magazine. "But I suppose Yves Saint Laurent is Jewish soap."

"What?"

"Let's leave this vale of tears," said Carla suddenly.

When they sat down in the kitchen, Carla held her head in

feigned agony. "I think if I hear 'Hark the Herald Angels Sing' one more time, I'm going to scream," she said. "The worst thing is the way Johnny goes out of his mind here. He won't talk to me and he won't talk to her. Jesus . . . let's talk about something else. Chrissy heard from Yale, I gather."

"Yes. She's been on cloud nine ever since, but she's funny. She told me she might transfer out her second term and go to Berkeley, I think it is . . . in California."

"What?"

"Well, between you and me, I think she wants to get farther away from home. Mom's been rough on her recently. She warns her about becoming a blue . . . blue . . ."

"Bluestocking?"

"That's it. She picks on her now more than me even. Mostly her clothes and her hair. She tells Chris about all the boy-friends *she* had back in high school and how if Chrissy just dedicates her life to academics, she's going to be an old maid and she'll never have children and grandchildren to love."

"And what does Chrissy say?"

"Chrissy tells her when she's thirty she's going to be unmarried and she's going to adopt six black kids and Mother just goes right out of her gourd."

Carla laughed. "And I bet she's still pushing U. Mass at you, right?"

"Yeah. She said not to listen to you about Sarah Lawrence."

"Of course. It's a shame they make you wait so long to hear though."

"I won't get into Sarah Lawrence, Carla. I know it."

"I think you will, Marsh. You know, it's funny. I don't really believe in predestination or anything, but I just have a feeling about this . . . I just have a feeling."

"I have a feeling I won't get in anywhere . . . except maybe Rollins. I wouldn't mind so much, it's near Shar."

"But you won't go there if you get into U. Mass, will you?"

"No, I guess not."

"And you won't go to U. Mass if you get into Sarah Lawrence. You wouldn't do that."

Marcia sighed. "I just don't know, Carla, I . . . "

"But you *couldn't,* Marsh. It'd be such a terrific chance to break out of all this provincialism up here. You'd meet dancers and writers and artists and I don't know . . . God! U. Mass— any state university is so average, so colorless. You'd be so bored. Sarah Lawrence could mean the beginning of a whole new life for you. Don't listen to Mother, Marsh, she—"

"I've seen it, Carla, when I went for my interview, and I must say it kind of scared me."

"Scared you!"

"Yes . . . well, the girls. They all looked so slinky and sophisticated and citified and I just got the feeling it would be so hard."

"That's Mother again I'm hearing. She went to Wheaton herself and it would kill her if you got into a better place. That's why she's so down on it. And she's prejudiced and so New *England.* Uptight, upright. She wouldn't know what Sarah Lawrence is all about anyway. She's just telling you to think those things, and they're all wrong."

"No," said Marcia slowly. "That's not the reason. She's trying to protect me. She doesn't want me to hope for Sarah Lawrence and then be disappointed."

Mother came striding into the kitchen. "Chrissy's agreed to play for us after all," she said. "What are you two doing here?"

"Digging into the goodies," said Carla, producing a cookie like a magician.

"Well, you have to get up now. Everybody come round the piano."

Mother ushered the family into the living room. She turned out the lights and lit candles. Grandfather and Grandmother Van Dam and Aunt Mim took their places beside Marcia and her father. Carla drew her chair back near Sharon and Buddy. Chrissy announced she hadn't played in some years and would probably make mistakes, but everyone said that was all right. Yes, she used to play so beautifully—she was too modest. John still sat in the dining room. "Come on, Johnny, we need you," Mother said, peering around the doorway just as Chrissy had begun "O Little Town of Bethlehem." Chrissy stopped abruptly. Marcia heard John throw down whatever it was he'd been reading and she saw his dark, supple shape saunter into the back of the room. He leaned against the wall with his hands in his pockets. Carla's eyes sought him out briefly and then gave up and stared stonily ahead. He wanted Chrissy to play, Marcia thought, but he won't sing himself.

Chrissy rocked left and right as she strained to hit the keys and read the music in the yellowed old book of Christmas carols. Mother's voice was crisp and on tune. It rose above Grandfather's and Grandmother's and Aunt Mim's and Marcia's father's, all of whom made a gallant effort to sing and remember the words. Sharon and Buddy made a show of singing, and only Carla and John, Marcia noticed, were silent.

The wind moaned softly around the house and banged a shutter rhythmically against one of the windows. A candle flickered briefly in a draft from the door. Marcia sang the words to all the old songs because she loved them and was not the least embarrassed by them. For one long instant, in the middle of "Joy to the World," she caught Mother's eye. Only after Mother's face turned back into the darkness did she realize

SEVENTEEN

there had been a small tear on the lash, and in the fathomless depth of that tear she understood that Mother loved her too but would never be able to show it. Perhaps it was only because she, Marcia, was singing and Mother's own two children fought her so and would not let her make the past be again.

Someone knocked on the door and then opened it. With a rush of cold air, the candles all guttered and went out. Although Marcia could not see him, she knew it was Raymond.

"So that was your sister."

"That was her."

Raymond turned up Willow Lane toward Woody's house and Woody's Christmas party. "She sure doesn't look like you," he said. "You're so . . . so much prettier."

"Oh, Raymie . . . thank you. Sharon used to be . . . well, she's gained so much weight and she's going to have another baby. I don't know what they're going to do. Buddy doesn't even . . . I guess I never liked Buddy. She probably shouldn't have married him. I was thinking that today, when—"

"Hey! what did you get for Christmas?"

"Oh, a couple of sweaters. Nothing much really. Carla gave me something nice though."

"Oh?"

"A book with a leather binding and gold stamped designs all over it. It's called *Portrait of the Artist as a Young Man.*"

"Boy, she's always giving you books. Can't she . . . doesn't she think there's anything else worth giving for Christmas?"

"Raymie, that's mean."

"I'm sorry. I was only kidding."

"No you weren't. You're just . . . " Marcia didn't finish her sentence. She wanted to say you're jealous of Carla, but Raymond would laugh at that. She had been so flattered by Carla's gift. She loved the soft morocco leather and the swirly, colored endpapers, but when she had read a few paragraphs, she knew she would never finish it, anymore than she had got beyond ten pages in *The Vicar of Wakefield,* and she knew Raymond had already guessed this.

Older brother Raymond—that's how he seemed to act toward Marcia, toward everyone in school still in her classes. Since he had graduated, all the people still in Raymond's old crowd at school were like so much weight off her shoulders. No time to make new friends. No time for anything except work, and Raymond, as much as she could fit him in. How am I going to do better in English this term? she asked herself. None of the people in Raymond's class who had gone to college came to the party. Marcia could tell this disappointed him. He kept looking at his watch and then out into the driveway. Was John Brogden back from Cornell? Yes, maybe. Bad weather. He must have been held up.

Somebody offered her a drink and she accepted and made a point of sipping at it. Someone had brought a baby to the party, Fay LoBiondo, now Fay something else, having married someone called Duke from the next town. The baby howled hopelessly.

"Give the kid some beer," someone suggested. Several people laughed.

"He's wet again," said Fay, putting down her drink impatiently. "The kid never stops, I swear to God."

The crying took an upswing into screaming. Fay went back into whatever room the baby was in. When she reappeared she said, "I picked him up and changed him and he just gets worse. Let him cry."

"Is he hungry?" Duke wanted to know.

"How should I know? He ate, didn't he?"

Marcia remembered the style of Fay's walk last year in the corridors of the high school. The jauntiness was still there, but it was tinged with alcohol and made Fay appear much older than her eighteen years.

"They had to get married, you know," said Raymond. He took Marcia by the hand and led her quickly away into the inevitable bedroom, guest room, spare room. Which room is this? Marcia asked herself, trying to remember the geography of Woody's house.

"I'm sorry," he said.

"Sorry? Why?" Marcia looked around at the bedroom he had chosen. A substantial mahogany dresser, too ugly to stay in another room, and a chipped iron bed covered with a hideous madras bedspread sat squarely in their respective corners, giving out not a sign of life.

"Jesus! It's so awful." Raymond said. "I hate this . . . sneaking away in people's houses. Next year it'll be different." When she turned away slightly he continued, "And them . . . Fay and her husband. I hate for you to see that. It makes me feel horrible. I . . . "

"Raymie, it's okay. They don't . . . they don't have anything to do with you and me." Marcia squinted with some irritation at the bare light bulb that hung in a torn paper shade above them. She switched off the light, not without smiling at him, trying to tell him without words that she would never be like Fay. She must put that thought out of her mind. They were not going to be married. She would not go to parties with Raymond next year, taking along a baby, drinking herself silly. She was going to college next year. She was going to go to Sarah Lawrence. She knew already somehow.

Sitting with her head pressed against Raymond's chest, she tried to expel some struggle from her mind. She wanted to put Chrissy and Carla and Mother all to rest for a while. Raymond didn't mind if she held him silently like this for five minutes, even an hour. She often did.

"It won't be like that for us," he whispered. "I promise it'll never be like that for us."

Us. Us meant next year. Marcia tried to ignore the word when he used it. She pictured it spelled with a capital *U*, like the capital *G* in God, but she could not bring herself to tell him there would be no Us, no next year. She had had an effect. She admitted it to herself when Raymond told her over and over again, last spring, last March—the first time they had made love. At the time she had felt she had practically restored sight to a blind Raymond. He had spoken so haltingly, "You are the one, the first one, the only one," he had said. She felt his patience now as he waited with his arms around her for some signal that she was with him, not in a classroom somewhere, not listening to Chrissy and Mother through the floor of her bedroom. "The one, the first one, the only one . . . you couldn't possibly know what it's like, but to go through your whole life . . . nobody ever in the world did anything to make me . . . happy. Even when I was a little kid, if I wanted to . . . if I tried to show someone . . . like my old man. One time they came and arrested him—my old man—and I kicked the cop. I must have been . . . I was just a little kid. The cop laughed and he took him away anyway, and my old man came back, he hadn't done it . . . they thought he'd done something . . . but he beat up on me for kicking that cop, and I was only . . . I screamed at him that I was only . . . I can't . . . You wouldn't believe what it's like to go for years and years without anybody. It's like there's nobody else in the world, even yourself after a while. Sometimes I think my whole life has gone by in a blur until I . . . met you. I . . . like nobody ever touched me or came near me . . . inside . . . me. I'm not making any sense, but . . . " But yes, she could imagine it very well, ever since her mother had died, and no, she wouldn't leave him ever. From heaviness to lightness he had gone that day in the back seat of somebody's Mercury Montego. Marcia didn't conjure up these words very often. They brought her quite close to tears except for the urgent, ungovernable excitement she also felt.

"Do you love me?" he asked, and she was brought back to the present room with the chipped iron bed. "Yes," she said. He took off his own clothes rapidly and then undressed her gently, as if she were a china doll. Marcia wished he wouldn't. She felt like ripping her own clothes off as fast as he did, but to say anything would have hurt him terribly. It was important that she let him undress her in this way, that she let him come to her, to "be the man" she sensed.

"Do you love me?" he asked again as he pulled the thin, ugly coverlet over both of them. "I love you," she said. I'm so happy, she told herself, and in the rush to her own completion she thought that yes, she did indeed love him.

"Merry Christmas."

"Merry Christmas."

"I have a present for you."

"Oh, Raymie, I left yours on the thing in the kitchen. I'm sorry."

"That's okay. That's okay. Here." He fumbled in the pocket of his jacket. As she sat up he draped the jacket over her shoulders. "Cold," he said.

Marcia held the little box, knowing what was in it before she opened it, recognizing the name of the local jewelry store on the lid, even in the dark.

"Don't say anything," he pleaded as she took the ring out and tried it cautiously on her little finger, not daring to put it on her ring finger and then have to take it off. "Don't say anything. Just keep it and put it away. It's not for now."

So she did and she watched him grin as she placed it carefully in her pocketbook. "I'll put it . . . I'll put it in the back compartment of my desk. She doesn't know about it," Marcia said. Where I keep my pills, she was about to add but thought better of it.

"She'd be upset?"

"She'd have a cow. Raymie?"

"Yes?"

"Thank you."

He's doing this for me, Marcia thought as he once again urged her gently down on the bed. For himself too, but he's doing this for me, and I'm just doing it for myself.

Eighteen

Marcia lay motionless on her bed. The late afternoon June sun poured stunningly through her window, warming her back. She heard the kitchen door slam and the noise of the vacuum cleaner stop.

"Chrissy? Where have you been? You said you were coming right home after school."

"Oh, Mom, I'm sorry. But it was just such a gorgeous day. The buttercups are out all over—here I brought you some— and Jenny wanted to take a ride over to the Matthew's house because they have a new litter of puppies and you should *see* them! They—"

"Chrissy, I want you to help Marcia."

"You mean about the test? What can she do about it now?"

"She's going to take it over. They're going to let her have another chance. Now I want you to help her."

"Well, she's got to ask me. I'm not going to—"

"She *will* ask you. She's promised to ask you. Now go on up there."

"All right already. I'm going."

The harsh whispers in the kitchen stopped, and Marcia could hear Chrissy's footsteps, deliberately heavy, on the stairs. She wouldn't make Chrissy come to her. She would have to go in, pencil and paper in hand, and ask—herself. She heard Chrissy sit down noisily at her desk and clear her throat expectantly.

"Chris?"

"Hi! How are you feeling?" Chrissy asked. She whirled around in her chair and greeted Marcia as if she hadn't seen her in years.

"Oh. Okay, I guess."

"What happened? I mean during the exam today I saw you just jump up and leave."

"I just made it to the ladies' room in time."

"Gee! Well, it sounds like . . . is it exciting to have an ulcer?"

Marcia laughed. "I feel like a businessman," she said.

Chrissy relaxed slightly. "Why?"

"Only businessmen are supposed to get ulcers . . . from tension and everything."

"But I thought Dr. Gordon said . . . Well, didn't Mom say you wouldn't get ulcers from tension at the age of eighteen?"

"Yeah, but I still feel like a businessman."

"Woman," prompted Chrissy.

"Businesswoman. Do businesswomen get ulcers?"

Chrissy thought about this for a moment. Marcia could tell she was weighing stereotypes, as she called them. In the end Chrissy could not decide whether ulcers were the result of men's craven inability to cope with day-to-day reality or a symptom of hard work and responsibility that all women should aspire to.

"Well, I thought you might help me with this poem . . . I . . . "

"Sure. Let's sit on the bed."

Mr. James, Marcia's English teacher, had decided through some incredible perversity to ignore the whole of the year's work and give as a final exam one poem, which the class had never read. At the beginning of the test, Marcia skimmed through it. It was totally incomprehensible to her. The worst of it was that she had studied for weeks, memorizing every question and answer in her Monarch Notes on the Romantic poets, on *King Lear* and *Julius Caesar*. She had prepared herself with the assiduity of setting a perfect dinner table. Everything—she could have answered everything today. All the facts were laid out in her mind like so many plates and forks and napkins waiting to be used. She looked around at the students already busily at work in their blue books. Chrissy's pilot English class at last. She recalled how surprised she had been in September when instead of easy Mrs. Forbes she had been assigned to Mr. James. Then she had looked at the mimeographed poem in front of her.

> That's my last Duchess painted on the wall,
> Looking as if she were alive. I call
> That piece a wonder, now; Frà Pandolph's hands
> Worked busily a day, and there she stands.
> Will't please you sit and look at her? I said
> "Frà Pandolph" by design, for never read
> Strangers like you that pictured countenance,
> The depth and passion of its earnest glance,
> But to myself they turned (since none puts by

The curtain I have drawn for you, but I)
And seemed as they would ask me, if they durst
How such a glance came there; so, not the first
Are you to turn and ask thus. Sir, 'twas not
Her husband's presence only, called that spot
Of joy into the Duchess' cheek; perhaps
Frà Pandolph chanced to say "Her mantle laps
Over my lady's wrist too much," or "Paint
Must never hope to reproduce the faint
Half-flush that dies along her throat:" such stuff
Was courtesy, she thought, and cause enough
For calling up that spot of joy. She had
A heart—how shall I say?—too soon made glad,

Halfway through the poem, Marcia had turned away and
looked out the window. The roses had just appeared that week.
She wished she could pick some, but they were school property
and she didn't dare. "Goneril, also desperately wanting Ed-
mund, sent Oswald to meet him at Gloucester's castle, not
knowing he had already left." She could dismiss that and the
rest of *King Lear* and every other thing she had studied from
her mind forever, if that were possible. She began reading the
poem again. No good. She started what she secretly called a
translation, for as far as she was concerned the poem might
as well have been written in German.

Realistic oil painting over there of a Duchess. Quite something, isn't it? F. P. worked hard, and there she is. Why don't
you sit down and look at it? I said . . . I said . . . F. P. by
design and never read? (come back to that part). Strangers like
you that pictured countenance . . . unknown people like
yourself that imagined a portrayal??? (come back to that later).

And so she had gone through the entire poem, losing the
thread every time she thought she'd picked it up. She had

handed in her blue book—empty—in the middle of the test and
had run out of the classroom. The rest of the day had dragged
on impossibly. At times Marcia felt the clock was actually going
backward. She hadn't the heart to see Raymond after school
for Cokes but had let him drive her home, promising to meet
him that night instead. She couldn't find the words to tell
Mother what had happened and had gone to her room and
lain down, saying she was not feeling well. As quietly as she
could manage, she had gotten sick over and over again in the
bathroom. She didn't want Mother to hear her, to ask worried
questions, to feel she had to hold her head or whatever it was
people held when somebody vomited. Exhausted, she pulled
the bedspread down and had tried to sleep. Sleep would not
come.

> *On behalf of the Committee of Admissions at Sarah
> Lawrence College, it gives me great pleasure to inform
> you that you have been accepted as a member of next
> year's freshman class, to begin the fall term in Sep-
> tember. This decision is subject to satisfactory com-
> pletion of your studies this year. We look forward ...*

"Satisfactory completion of your studies this year," and Mr.
James had been so kind. At four-thirty, the telephone had rung.
Mother had said, "Yes, yes . . . I understand. That's terribly
nice of you. Wait till I tell her. She's been so depressed I
haven't been able to get a word out of her. Yes, and thank you,
Mr. Sisson."

"Marcia?"

"Who was that?"

"Marcia, that was Mr. Sisson."

"What did he want?"

"Marcia, he told me Mr. James said you wrote absolutely
nothing in your blue book in the English final today."

"That's right, Mother. I couldn't tell you, I . . . "

Mother picked Marcia's hand up off the bed and patted it reassuringly, although her own voice was more anxious than Marcia's. "It's going to be all right. It's going to be all right. The school knows you haven't been well. Mr. Sisson says there's a waiting list at Sarah Lawrence, that you'd probably be put back to the waiting list and maybe not get in at all, but Mr. James is going to give you another chance tomorrow."

"What? The same test?"

"Apparently yes. He said something to Mr. Sisson about understanding the poem. . . was it? A poem?"

"A poem."

"He said something about understanding it being more important . . . I don't know what he said, but you're to study it again and get a good night's sleep and take the test first thing in the morning. The school is so proud of you . . . You've come so far, Marcia . . . it's just unbelievable. Mr. Sisson said it would be ridiculous to let one exam trip you up now, especially since you were sick. I think it was your college boards last time that did it. He said he's never seen such an improvement in all his years as a guidance counselor. I think if you asked Chris when she gets home, she'd help you . . . if you need help."

Marcia had said nothing. She nodded seriously, incredulously at Mother's words. All the fear for nothing now. Mother had made it go away like magic. She would simply do it again, she would simply ask Chrissy what the poem meant.

> Too easily impressed; she liked whate'er
> She looked on, and her looks went everywhere.
> Sir, 'twas all one! My favor at her breast,
> The dropping of the daylight in the West,
> The bough of cherries some officious fool

Broke in the orchard for her, the white mule
She rode with round the terrace—all and each
Would draw from her alike approving speech,
Or blush at least. She thanked men,—good! but
      thanked
Somehow—I know not how—as if she ranked
My gift of a nine-hundred-years-old name
With anybody's gift. Who'd stoop to blame
This sort of trifling? Even had you skill
In speech—(which I have not)—to make your will
Quite clear to such an one, and say, "Just this
Or that in you disgusts me; here you miss,
Or there exceed the mark"—and if she let
Herself be lessoned so, nor plainly set
Her wits to yours, forsooth, and made excuse
—E'en then would be some stooping; and I choose
Never to stoop. Oh sir, she smiled, no doubt,
Whene'er I passed her; but who passed without
Much the same smile? This grew; I gave commands;
Then all smiles stopped together. There she stands
As if alive. Will't please you rise? We'll meet
The company below, then, I repeat
The Count your master's known munificence
Is ample warrant that no just pretence
Of mine for dowry will be disallowed;
Though his fair daughter's self, as I avowed
At starting, is my object. Nay, we'll go
Together down, sir. Notice Neptune, though,
Taming a sea-horse, thought a rarity,
Which Claus of Innsbruck cast in bronze for me!

"Now that's pretty clear."
"Chris, I'm sorry. I . . . "

"Okay. Let's start at the beginning."

"All right."

"Now . . . the speaker, the person who's talking . . . he's a Duke. He's negotiating with an envoy for the hand ,of the Count's daughter."

"Where does it say that?"

"Well, look. My last *Duchess*. Who's married to a Duchess? A Duke, right? And here 'The Count your master'—this guy is representing the Count. 'Known munificence'—that means generosity."

"I know what the word means."

"Okay, okay . . . 'munificence is ample warrant that no just pretence of mine for dowry will be disallowed.' So he wants to marry the Count's daughter. Right?"

"I guess so."

"But he killed his last wife."

"Where does it say *that*?"

"Look at all this bit in the middle. 'She ranked my gift of a nine-hundred-years-old name with anybody's gift.' She didn't appreciate him, in other words . . . then here 'This grew, I gave commands; then all smiles stopped together.' He had her put to death . . . all smiles stopped together. Easy!" Chrissy snapped the book shut.

"Gee," said Marcia.

"You're a lucky stiff. You know that. Jamsey's going to let you take it over. He thinks you were sick."

"I *was* sick."

"I know you were, Marsh, but . . . you know what I mean."

Marcia went back into her own room and sat at her desk. She stared at the poem one more time. Slowly the words regained the configurations that had confounded her before. It would be all right, of course. She would remember, tomorrow, how Chrissy had explained the poem. She would be able to fudge the essay, at least enough for a B, but what of the next exam, and the next? When would the next "My Last Duchess" ambush her like a would-be assassin? At Sarah Lawrence there would likely be no Mr. Sissons with their pride resting on the number of graduates to go on to college. And Mother had been so proud. Carla had literally jumped up and down. Marcia could hear over the telephone. Sarah Lawrence. That was just as good as Yale, Carla'd said again and again. Just as good, and Marcia had *done* it. She, Marcia, had slipped in by means of some miracle, and another miracle today had given her a reprieve. This must be some form of predestination, as Carla had said. Marcia closed her book. Never, never in her whole life did she want to read a book again. Fourteen minutes to nine. Raymond would be waiting.

She reached back into the secret cubbyhole in her desk. The little box was there—undisturbed. She slipped the ring on her finger and went downstairs and out the front door unnoticed.

Raymond had parked a long way down the block, as Marcia had instructed him, in case Mother made a fuss about her going out after failing an exam. Marcia walked quickly, wondering if he would lift his head and see her—if, by chance, his headlights would catch a facet of the diamond on her left hand and let him know before she told him, but he was absorbed in something. *Car and Driver* magazine. It had been lying on the seat of the car that afternoon.

Marcia started to run. She could already hear the voices, Mother's and even Carla's, through the floor.

"Why? why? why did she do it? She could have gone to Sarah Lawrence. Anywhere! Even the University of Massachusetts wouldn't have been so bad. She had everything ahead of her."

"Don't ask me. She talked to you a lot more than she talked to me. Didn't she say anything? Didn't she at least give some

reason for getting married? You could talk to her. You could make sense of her."

Marcia felt a tug in her stomach. The deep silent pool inside, she thought. It's nothing but a stomach full of ulcers! She ran downstairs in her imagination. *"Because,"* she said right out to them. *"Because we're in love. Isn't that enough?"*

The familiar pain engulfed her for a moment, but she kept on running as if it were not there at all.